To: Rosies,

Thank-you for your support.
I wish you have a great holiday
season.

Peace.

A Model

For Murder

A Novel

Roy A. Teel Jr.

A Model for Murder

A Novel

Roy A. Teel Jr.

The Iron Eagle Series: Book Five

An Imprint of Narroway Publishing LLC.

Narroway Publishing LLC.
Imprint: Narroway Press
P.O. Box 1431
Lake Arrowhead, California 92352

This is a work of fiction. Names, characters, places, and incidents either are the product of the author's imagination or are used fictitiously, and any resemblance to actual persons, living or dead, business establishments, events or locales is entirely coincidental.

First Edition

ISBN: 978-0-9903637-1-2

Teel, Roy A., 1965-
   A Model for Murder, The Iron Eagle Series: Book Five /
   Roy A. Teel Jr. — 1st ed. — Lake Arrowhead, Calif. Narroway Press
   c2015. p. ; cm. ISBN: 978-0-9903637-1-2 (Hardcover)

1. Hard-Boiled – Fiction. 2. Police, FBI – Fiction. 3. Murder – Fiction.
4. Serial Killers – Fiction. 5. Mystery – Fiction. 6. Suspense – Fiction.
7. Graphic Violence – Fiction. 8. Graphic Sex – Fiction.
   Title.

         Book Editing: Finesse Writing and Editing LLC.
         Cover and Book Design: Adan M. Garcia, FSi studio
         Author Photo: F. E. Arnest

"This novel is dedicated to those who have been victims of the ruthless, the heartless, and the vile. For those with little hope, hope is out there, and sometimes it's in the last place you would expect!"

Roy A. Teel Jr.

Also by Roy A. Teel Jr.

Nonfiction:

*The Way, The Truth, and The Lies: How the Gospels
Mislead Christians about Jesus' True Message*

Against the Grain: The American Mega-church and its Culture of Control

Fiction:

The Light of Darkness: Dialogues in Death: Collected Short Stories

And God Laughed, A Novel

Fiction Novel Series:

Rise of the Iron Eagle: Book One

Evil and the Details: Book Two

Rome Is Burning: Book Three

Operation Red Alert: Book Four

"The sexual abuse and exploitation of children is one of the most vicious crimes conceivable, a violation of mankind's most basic duty to protect the innocent."

—James T. Walsh

ƑEAL OF THE IRON EAGLE. ®

Table of Contents

CHAPTER ONE

"This is a game changer...this sicko killed one
of our own. Hell is about to be unleashed."

I t was just past midnight, and Terry Brady and her lover, Hillary Sums, had taken off for a late night run to clear their heads. They decided to run around the Hollywood reservoir and were just crossing onto the reservoir dam while chatting. Terry had slowed her pace, so Hillary slowed with her, and they stopped in the middle of the dam for a rest. The lights of Los Angeles looked like stars far below them, and they took in the romantic scene holding each other's hands. Terry got her breath back, and the two started walking, admiring the view, and talking about the argument that had brought them out of their home and into the darkness. They were just crossing to the other end of the dam when Terry spotted something in the water near the edge. They both wore running lights on sweatbands on their heads, and they shined the light into the watery edges between the concrete dam and the lakeside and saw a human arm floating in the water. Hillary let out a scream, and Terry pulled her cell phone to call for help.

Jim O'Brian was fast asleep with Barbara wrapped around him when his cell phone rang. He moved to untangle himself from his wife while searching through the darkness for the flashing light and loud ringtone. "What?" He was lying in bed with the phone to his ear listening. Barbara got up and went into the bathroom, slamming the door behind her. Jim told the caller to wait, and he yelled, "I'm on the GODDAMNED PHONE HERE!" Barbara yelled back, "NO FUCKING SHIT…AND I HAVE TO PISS!" He shook his head and told the caller to continue. He hung up the phone and was out of bed rummaging for his clothes on the floor when the bathroom door opened, flooding the room with light. Barbara was standing nude in the bathroom doorway with her hands on her hips. "So, what is it tonight, Jimmy?" He was pulling on his underwear as he responded. "A body in the LA reservoir. They need me on scene." He had gotten his pants on and was slipping into his t-shirt when Barbara walked to the closet and grabbed him a fresh sheriff's shirt and t-shirt. "The pants are okay, but put these on. They're freshly pressed. I want my husband looking like a sheriff not a bum." He laughed and took the clothing from her and finished dressing.

"I thought when you became sheriff these late night calls would stop," Barbara said, sitting down on her side of the bed with her back to Jim. "When they call me, Barb, you know it's a big ass deal. I have to go out there. I'm sorry." She rolled back into bed and pulled the covers over her head. "I have to work in the morning." "I know, Barb. I know." She threw the covers down revealing her bare breasts and asked, "We have more money than God! John and Sara have more money than God. Why the FUCK are we still doing this shit? I want to retire!" Jim leaned in and kissed each breast and then her lips and said, "You are one sexy woman, Barb. One hell of a sexy woman. We will retire as soon as my term as Sheriff of Los Angeles County is up. We already agreed to that. I have announced that I will not run for a second term, but I do have two more years to go, my dear." "Fuck the politics of it. Let's just roll it up and move away from this shit before one of us gets killed." Jim looked on and said, "We can talk about this later, Barb. I have to get going." He was walking out the bedroom door when she said, "I hope to FUCK they woke John. I know he will end up out there, too." She threw a pillow at Jim's back as he left the room and the house.

Jim wasted no time calling John's cell phone before he was even in his car. "Swenson." "You're not asleep?" "Um…no. I'm in my truck headed to the Hollywood dam. Where are you?" Jim was starting his car and said with disdain, "In my fuckin' car headed to the same fuckin' place you are. Who called you?" "LAPD." Jim pulled out onto the freeway headed for the dam. "Why the fuck would LAPD call the FBI directly? This is my jurisdiction." John laughed. "I don't know. Meet you on the dam?" "Yea." Jim hung up the phone, turned on his sirens and lights, and headed for the dam.

Jim pulled up to the scene and not only was John already there so was the coroner. He got out of his car and headed for the well-lit area where a yellow tarp was half in the water. Jade Morgan was yelling out instructions to her team, and John was standing near her when Jim approached. "Let me fuckin' guess. Teen female victim, breasts gnawed to shit?" Jade nodded. "Where's the media? They are usually all over this shit." John pointed to the two women that found the body. Jim recognized them right away. "You've got to be fuckin' kidding me...they found the body?" John nodded, and Jim said, "Oh, I have to interview them!" John followed behind him saying, "I thought you might!" Jim walked up and said, "Well, if it isn't the two biggest pain in my ass reporters in Los Angeles. What's the deal, Hill? You and Terry found this victim?" They nodded saying nothing. "What's the problem, ladies? You two are never short on words when you're reporting bullshit on the news. Where's the investigative reporter team now?" John put his hand on Jim's shoulder and said, "Please...let's not start this now." "Start what, John? You know as well as I do that these two are going to sensationalize this situation, and by the time the news airs, they will have this plastered over all the major networks with some god awful bunch of lying bullshit. Fuck...of all the people to find this poor kid." John pulled him back and said, "Let me talk to them."

As John leaned in to speak to the women, he heard a familiar voice call to him from the distance. "Special Agent John Swenson FBI?" John turned to see LAPD Detective Randy Strom walking toward the scene. Jim saw Strom coming and said, "Oh, this ain't gonna be fuckin' good." "What's the FBI doing here, John? This is my crime scene," Strom said. "I was called in by Rampart. I don't know the reasons yet. I just arrived and was preparing to question the witnesses who found the body." Strom looked over at Jim and asked, "And what the fuck are you doing here, O'Brian? You doing some late night slumming?" "Fuck you, Randy. I was home in bed with my wife when I got a call from one of your people so cut the shit. You're standing in a multijurisdictional crime scene, and the overriding power is that of the FBI." Strom flipped Jim off and stood next to John as he questioned the women.

"Okay, so that we all get off on the right foot here, you two aren't reporters right now. Right now, you are witnesses to a homicide. Are we clear?" John's towering figure was clearly intimidating Hillary and Terry. They nodded. "So... what brings you ladies onto the dam at this hour of the morning?" The women explained their situation. John looked on and asked, "Did you see anyone other than the victim?" They both shook their heads. "Did either of you go down to the water and get near the victim?" Once again, both woman shook their heads. Jim couldn't help himself, "Who was eating out who when the fight started, or who refused to munch the other's carpet?" John slugged him in the arm while Randy just rolled his eyes as the two women stood doe-eyed.

Jade called out to John, and he walked over to her, leaving Randy and Jim with the women. "This one is brutal, John." Jade said with a sense of sadness in her voice. "They're all brutal, Jade." She shook her head and said, "No, the killer is increasing his brutality. I won't know more until I can get her on the table, but based on my preliminary crime scene observations this little girl was killed with some type of acid." John looked over to the yellow tarp and said, "Show me." The girl was lying on her back, ready to be placed in a body bag. Her eyes were wide open, her skin a pale blue. Her lips were parted, and there was a hole in her throat from the bottom of her lower jaw down to the beginning of the sternum. John grabbed a flashlight and a pair of latex gloves and asked Jade for a cotton swab. She handed it to him, and he ran it across the opening in her throat then lifted it to his nose. He pulled it away instantly. "Ammonia!" He handed the swab to Jade, who sniffed it as well then put it in a bag to go to the lab. "Drain cleaner?" she asked, looking at the girl's solemn expression. "Hard to say. It's not the only compound that she drank, but someone went to great lengths to kill this kid," John said as he stood up. Jade motioned to David Markham, her deputy medical examiner, to zip up the bag.

John walked back over to Randy and Jim who were still arguing back and forth over jurisdiction. "HEY!" John yelled, "It's my jurisdiction, so you two can knock it off." Randy stormed off in the direction of Jade, and Jim laughed. "So what did Jade want?" "Me to look at the body before she bagged it for the morgue." "Why?" John took a deep breath and looked out over the city lights from the top of the dam. "This is a new manner of killing." "A different killer?" Jim asked, and John shook his head. "New manner of execution. He still ground off her breasts, but it looks like he killed her by forcing her to drink some type of acid. It ate a hole right through her esophagus and neck." Jim was just about to say something when they heard a loud blood curdling scream coming from the scene.

The two men went running to see Randy on his knees in front of the body screaming and calling out a name. "Suzy…Suzy…oh God…oh my God!" Jim and John looked at each other then at Randy on his knees over the corpse now in a body bag with just the face exposed. John knelt down next to Randy and asked, "Do you know her?" Randy was hyperventilating, and John grabbed a vomit bag from Jade and handed it to him. He put the bag to his face, and he started to breath into it then started to vomit. Jade had ordered the body placed on a gurney to take back to the lab, but Randy grabbed the bag and wouldn't let go. "My baby…oh dear God, not my baby!" John and Jim pulled him back away from Jade, so the body could be moved, and Jim looked at Randy and asked, "Please don't tell me that she's your child." Randy couldn't speak. He was all over the scene, and John and Jim had to restrain him from contaminating the area and requested a medic to sedate him. They got him into an ambulance that had been called to the scene and gave him an injection. When he started to get his composure, John put his hand on Randy's shoulder and asked, "Is that your child?" He nodded slowly and deliberately.

Jim walked back away from Randy and John with his hands in his pockets. The women stood off in the distance. Hillary had her cell phone out and was talking on it. Jim rushed her and grabbed the phone from her hand. "This is not just any other GODDAMN CRIME SCENE, YOU BITCH!" He threw the phone on the ground, smashing it to pieces. "Show some goddamn respect…" He sat down on the edge of a railing overlooking the dam and LA in the distance. He looked over at John with his arm on Randy's shoulder. He said while facing the women, "This is a game changer…this sicko killed one of our own. Hell is about to be unleashed." John motioned to Jim to come back over. He looked at the two women and said, "Don't move. Don't budge. Don't so much as sneeze until I clear you to leave this scene." He walked slowly over to Randy and John mumbling to himself, "I'm walking into a father's worst nightmare."

CHAPTER TWO

*"We've got a psychopath on our hands, and I
don't know how we're going to catch him."*

Alan Holden held a Nikon camera while giving instructions to his young model near the pier in Santa Monica. It was seven fifteen a.m., and he wanted to take advantage of the morning sunlight before it was too intrusive. "Holly, honey, I want you to be more carefree. Move with the wind and the music of the sea." Holly Bachman had just turned sixteen and had been modeling for Alan for over two years. He discovered her at a mall beauty pageant and turned her into one of the most recognizable faces in Hollywood and the world. "I know what you want, Alan...I'm just tired. I have to be back in New York tonight for a late night talk show about my new movie." Alan nodded and said sweetly, "I know honey; I know. Just give me ten minutes. I know we can get the right shots. Remember, this is for *Sixteen* magazine and is going to be your cover shot for your new movie." She smiled a faint smile then turned on her charisma, and he was able to get the shots he wanted. Alan let the camera hang down after the last shot and said, "Perfect, angel. You did perfect. I will get these over to the magazine after breakfast. Are you hungry?" She nodded emphatically, and he took her to a little breakfast spot in Santa Monica for a nice meal.

They snuck in under the radar and sat with two huge breakfasts. "How can you eat all of that food and still keep that amazing figure?" "I don't have an eating disorder, Alan. Believe it or not, I have a fast metabolism. That's what running from boys and the paparazzi will do for you." He laughed and said, "No one believes you're only sixteen. They swear that you are in your mid-twenties." She laughed with a mouth full of pancakes. "That's partly genetics and partly your fault, Alan. Working with you has aged me." Holly was mature for her age; she had the build of an adult and the intellect to match it. "Yea, well, someone had to nurture you. You weren't getting it at home. I have made it my pet project to love and protect you no matter how much fame you have." She laughed again, and the two finished their breakfast then fought off the throngs of onlookers who spotted her. The cameras were clicking at Holly as she smiled and signed autographs all the way to Alan's car. She dove in the front seat and said, "Sleep. Please, Alan. I will give you anything you want. Just let me get a few hours sleep before I leave for New York." He smiled at her as he sped down PCH to the 10 Freeway and the 405 to his home off 5th Avenue on an access road below the Getty Museum.

He pulled into the gated home and got Holly into bed in the guest house that she lived in when she was not on the road. Back in the main house, he uploaded the pictures from the morning shoot and sent them to the magazine in an email. Alan had noticed when he came into the house that one of his weapons was missing from its wall display in the living room, but he had a good idea where it was. He walked out past the swimming pool and tennis court to a small green building, unlocked the doors, turned on the lights, and rummaged around in an old metal container looking for the weapon. There was a steel table in the middle of the room with two holes in the top and leather straps. Under the table were three separate motors. One was a weed eater that a gardener would use, but it had steel wire instead of the usual plastic string. The other motor was mounted to an industrial food processor under the table with a rack of interchangeable blades; and, finally, the third motor connected to a meat grinder. All three were mounted onto a round steel disc.

He found the weapon nestled between the motors and pressed a button that made the steel circle turn, so he could get to it. He grabbed it and took it out of the shed with him. It glistened in the late morning sunlight: a stainless steel machete with a long black leather wrapped handle. Alan looked at the sleek steel and said, "Why the hell isn't this hanging with my collection?" He walked back into the house and re-hung it, then undressed, showered, and began preparing to shave and get ready for the day. He had no sooner lathered up when Holly came walking into the bathroom nude and rubbing her eyes. "I can't sleep, Alan...I'm so tired, but I can't sleep. Can I lie in your bed?" He nodded as he shaved his face, and she disappeared into the bedroom. She returned with the machete in her hand, waving it wildly. He grabbed her wrist and said, "It's not a toy, Holly. One wrong move and you could cut yourself really, really badly. Why did you pull it off the wall?" "I was wandering around and saw that you put it back up, and I wanted to hold it." Alan slowly took the blade away and carried it back and put it in its wall holder. Holly skulked off to the bedroom while he finished cleaning himself up.

Alan walked back into the bedroom to find Holly lying on her stomach on the bed. Her nude white skin glistened from the glitter powder she used all over. She was pretending to sleep, and he reached his hand out and touched her on the ass. "You know you want to fuck me, Alan. When are we going to do it?" She rolled over; his penis was erect, and she reached out and caressed it. She slid over to the side of the bed and went down on him. He didn't resist, and they spent the rest of the day in bed.

Jim made it back to his office, which had been relocated back to the state building in downtown LA. He walked in to see Belinda Ferguson typing away on her computer. "Are you doing my dictation?" Jim asked. "As always…I have your midi recorder if you need it." He shook his head and walked into his office. He closed the door and opened the window next to his desk, took a cigarette out of the pack, lit it, and flipped his Zippo closed. He took a few hits off the smoke before he heard Belinda yell, "No smoking in the building, Sheriff. You know what happened the last time." He took a few more deep hits before putting it out. Belinda was referring to a surprise visit by members of the Los Angeles County Board of Supervisors who caught him smoking in his spot. He caught the wrath of hell for it.

Jim walked over to his desk and opened the case file on Suzy Strom. The autopsy reports were in it, and he read through them as he waited for his midi recorder to be returned. His office phone rang, and it was John. "Yea!" "Did you get the reports on Strom's daughter?" "Yea, John. I just started to look them over." "The killer has raised the bar. He used a sulfuric acid drain cleaner on the kid." Jim was reading the report and asked, "Does the Eagle have any leads on this guy?" There was silence on the other end of the line. Jim frowned and asked, "Do YOU have any leads on this guy?" "Nothing. This one is a real ghost. He's getting more brazen in his killings, and he's definitely killing in some remote location. But the M.O. is all over the place. I have been profiling this guy since the third killing, and just when I think I have him figured out, he changes tactics." Jim laughed. "Well, he might change the method of execution for his victims, but he still mutilates their breasts and pussies." "Jesus, Jim! Vagina. Vagina or vaginal area. These are kids.

Why do you have to be so damn vulgar?" John was pissed. "Yea, yea. Old enough to bleed, old enough to butcher, John. Ever heard that before? This guy grabs them young, rapes them, and then mutilates them. He doesn't want them too old, and he doesn't want them too young. We've got a psychopath on our hands, and I don't know how we're going to catch him." There were a few moments of silence then John said, "I'm going out to interview the Stroms this afternoon. You want to tag along?" Jim checked to see if his calendar was clear. "Yea...what time?" "One p.m." Jim looked over at the clock on the wall; it was half past twelve. "Where do they live?" "Santa Monica. I spoke to Randy about an hour ago. He and his wife, Amy, will be there." "Okay. What's the address?" John gave him the information, and Jim said, "I will meet you at the house." There was a pause then Jim continued, "Did you see the news this morning?" "Yea!" John said angrily. Jim said, "I told you those bitches would turn this into a sensationalized story. Fuckin' cunts...I hate those two, John. I really, really hate those two. They prey on the weak, the feeble, and the dying. They go out of their way to make the lives of victims more of a hell than they already are." John cleared his throat, "I agree that they go over the top, and they did with this story, but it's a First Amendment issue, Jim." "Oh yea? What if these two were around when Amber was murdered and did what they are doing to Randy and Amy and the other victims of the Hollywood Killer? Wouldn't you feel like you were victimized by their shit stories?" John paused before saying, "I see your point...but there's nothing we can do about it. They have protection under the First Amendment." "Until that fucker gets one or both of them," Jim said in a sadistic way. "They're not his type plus they're too old. Plus...they're the ones who made this killer famous. It's been the biggest news story since the fires and the president's abduction last year." "I'll see you at Randy's." Jim hung up the phone.

"Belinda, I need my midi recorder," he bellowed through the closed door. She walked in and handed it to him with the dictated reports. "What would I do without you?" "I would say 'get fired for not doing your reports,' but you're an elected official, so I would just say 'be lost.'" She smiled as she handed him the recorder then walked out. "You know, I had my eye on you before Barbara and I got back together." She walked back into his doorway and said, "Well, if you did you never did anything about it, did you?" He shook his head. "Knowing Barbara as well as I do, and knowing your temper, you would never have had a shot with me!" He laughed as she walked out the door and went back to her desk.

John's truck was parked in front of the Strom residence when Jim pulled up. The house was immaculate and directly across the street from the ocean. He parked and walked up to the front door, and the door opened before he could ring the bell, and Randy was standing there staring at him. "What are you doing here?" Randy asked with a seething anger in his voice. "John asked me to come down and work with him on the case. Look, Randy, I know we have had our differences, but I'm here as the Sheriff of LA County. I'm here to try and find the animal that did this to your daughter." He let Jim in and led him into the living room where John and Amy were sitting. "Mrs. Strom, I would like to introduce you to Sheriff Jim O'Brian." She looked half heartedly at him and said, "I know Jim." She invited him to sit, and he pulled out his midi recorder and sat down on a chair next to the couch. John was on the other side of her, and Randy came over and sat between Amy and Jim. John had his tablet out and asked, "You mentioned that you had an unusual encounter with a man at Zuma Beach a few weeks ago?"

"Yes…um…Suzy and I had gone to the beach, so she could do some body surfing. I was approached by a man who said he was a modeling agent and wanted to know if I or Suzy had ever done any modeling." "How did the conversation evolve?" "I really don't remember. I just recall that Suzy had brought me some stuff from the car, and then he was behind me." Jim asked, "Can you give us a description of the man? Did he give you a name?" Amy looked over at Jim and said, "He gave me a business card. I gave it to Agent Swenson. He was a handsome young man, probably mid-thirties, well-dressed, dark hair and eyes. I went to his website after our meeting on the beach. There is a photograph of him on the site as well as all the models he represents. He is well-respected in modeling from what I understand. He even represents Holly Bachman." Jim had a blank look on his face. John told him she was a famous teenage model, singer, and actress.

John asked both Amy and Randy, "Do you know if Suzy ever contacted…" He looked down at the business card that Amy had handed him, "Mr. Holden?" She shook her head. "She didn't even know who he was. He handed me the card. I never gave it to Suzy." "Did she know he was a modeling agent and photographer?" She looked around half dazed, "Um…he said something about it as we were driving away, but I put the brakes on that right away, and I'm the only one who had his card." Jim and John looked over at Randy, and before either one could ask he stood up and said, "Come on. I will show you to Suzy's room." The three men walked back to the front foyer and up the stairs. Randy opened a door and entered with John and Jim behind him. Jim looked around and asked, "Has anyone searched the room?" "Yea…I had my detectives do a search, but it came up empty. They didn't find anything." John was putting on a pair of latex gloves and said, "Randy, you know that you can't be involved in this investigation. You have a conflict of interest." He nodded slowly. "If you or your people contaminated this room, you could compromise the whole investigation."

"God damn you, Swenson...my fuckin' kid is on the coroner's slab right now, and you want me to give a shit about rules?" John looked him square in the eye and said, "Yes, Randy, I do. I've been where you and Amy are right now. I know what you're going through. You can't run on adrenaline and a hunger for revenge. If you do, you will mess up the whole case, and Suzy might end up a cold case file in all of our offices." Randy stepped back into the doorway. John looked at him and said, "You might want to wait outside. I'm going to tear this room apart looking for clues." Randy looked up at John towering over him. "Word around the department is you have been hunting for the Iron Eagle." John nodded. "There's also a rumor that you or Jim knows who the Eagle is!" John slowly shook his head, staring at Randy. "You do what you must to find this bastard, but you better hope that you find him before I or the Iron Eagle does because I won't turn this sick bastard over to police. I will take care of him myself." Jim said calmly, "I understand your desire for justice, Randy. John and I are going to forget that you ever said that. Let us do our job. No one is going to do anything to this guy until we find and nail him." Randy turned and walked out of the room.

Jim and John spent two hours tearing the room apart. They were about to give up when John noticed a small slip of paper between the box spring and mattress of Suzy's bed. He reached down and pulled it out to find that it was Holden's business card. "Well," John said, holding the card between his fingers. "Holden did get to her." He flipped the card over, and there was some writing on the back. John handed the card to Jim and asked, "Her writing or Holden's?" "Definitely Suzy's writing. Looks like we have an address to follow up on." Jim handed John back the card and asked, "Are you going to tell Randy and Amy?" He shook his head. "Not yet. Let's check this guy out and check out this address. I don't want to give Randy a reason to do something crazy. I know what grief can do to you." Jim nodded and said, "Yea...so does Walter Cruthers!" John didn't respond. He worked with Jim to put the room back together as best they could and went back downstairs to join Amy and Randy.

"Did you find anything?" Amy asked. John looked into her red teary eyes and said, "Maybe...we are going to follow up on the guy who gave you his card and check him out." Randy stood up quickly and asked, "Do you think there's a connection between him and Suzy?" John motioned to Randy to calm down. "No...Randy. We don't know that there is any link. It's nothing more than a lead and possibly a person of interest. The last thing anyone wants to do is jump to conclusions, that's how innocent people get hurt." Randy sat back down as Jim and

John showed themselves out. They got to the street, and Jim walked over to John at his truck and asked, "What's your gut telling you?" John looked across the street to the sea while answering. "It's telling me we need to look at this guy, that's all. If he is as reputable as Amy claims, it might be a dead end or maybe he knows something about Suzy that will lead us to her killer." Jim took a cigarette out of his top left pocket, stuck it in his mouth, and lit it. "Well, work your magic, John, then let me know when we are going to pay Mr. Holden a visit." Jim turned and walked back to his car and drove off. John punched Holden's information into his computer in his truck and waited for the results as he drove down PCH headed back to his office.

Alan Holden was sitting up in bed with Holly lying next to him. She was teary eyed and got up and walked to the bathroom. There was a small amount of blood running down her thighs. Alan got up and walked into the bathroom behind her and said, "I didn't know you were a virgin, Holly. I thought you were kidding about me being your first." She was wiping the tears from her face with a wash cloth as she responded, "It's not your fault, Alan. I never told you. I have wanted you to be my first since we met. I just didn't know it would hurt so much. You're my first lover. No one has ever done the things you did to me. I have heard of anal sex, but I had no idea it would hurt so much." He walked up behind her and wrapped his arms around her. "I didn't mean to hurt you. All you had to do was say stop." She nodded and kissed his arm and smiled a teary smile and said, "Well, I'm not a virgin anymore. In any of my holes, I'm a woman." She turned to him and kissed his face and asked if she could use his shower. He nodded, and she got in and took a long hot one.

When she got out, he handed her a towel and asked, "What time is your flight?" "Five." He looked at the clock in the bathroom; it was three. "Well, my dear, you need to get dressed and make sure you are all packed. I will drop you off at LAX, and I will fly out to be with you in a few days. I have some shoots to finish up here." She nodded and smiled. The tears had left her eyes. She hugged him and said, "Thank you for being my first lover. I learned a lot. Can we do it again in New York?" He hugged her back and said, "Yes…but you are under age. You can't tell anyone about this, or I will get in a lot of trouble. I could go to jail." Holly got a horrified look on her face. "Oh my God! Just for making love to me?" He nodded. "You have to be eighteen, honey. You are two years shy of that, so it is very, very important that this remains our secret forever." She nodded and said, "It will remain our secret, but when I'm eighteen I'm going to tell the world that you are my lover!" He smiled and said, "You can do that then, but you can still never tell anyone we had sex for the first time when you were sixteen." She kissed him and ran off to her house to get her things.

Alan stood looking in the mirror at himself naked. He wiped the fog off the mirror from Holly's shower, and a huge smile broke across his face. "I've been wanting to fuck you since I met you…it was a nice rush, Holly, a nice rush, but nothing compared to the others." He jumped in the shower, dressed, then got Holly and her bags and took her to LAX. She said, "I will see you in New York." "You bet you will." She looked him in the eye and said, "I love you, Alan." "I love you, too, Holly." She held his arm tight and said, "No…I LOVE YOU, ALAN!" He kissed her cheek and said, "I know, sweetheart. Now get through security. Your private jet flights cost me a fortune." He laughed as did she, and he watched as she disappeared into the private terminal at LAX, a paparazzi-free zone where celebrities could travel in peace if they had the money to do it. He looked at his watch, and his eyes got huge. "I have a date…" He took off and headed to the 405 Freeway.

Ally Morrison was standing at the corner of Sunset and Vine where the photographer told her to be. She was dressed in a short skirt and low cut top. Her breasts were on parade, and the catcalls from passing motorists and others on the street were scaring her. She was just getting ready to leave when her cell phone rang. "Hello? Oh, hi, it's you. Where are you? I'm waiting where you told me to wait." There were a few moments of silence, and she started to walk down Hollywood Boulevard with the phone to her ear. She was listening as she walked until she came to an alley where she turned and disappeared into the darkness.

CHAPTER THREE

"If he's a killer, he has one hell of a front going. His
modeling and talent agency is real, and it's impressive."

John got the report on Holden, and he was clean, not even a traffic ticket. He drove to the address on his business card in Los Angeles, 2121 Avenue of the Stars. He parked his truck in the circular parking area outside the building's main parking structure and showed his ID to the security guard. He walked into the building and looked at the electronic building directory. He typed Alan Holden's name into the computer and found his suite number, 2100. He showed his ID at the security desk, and they opened an express elevator for him to the twenty-first floor. When the elevator doors opened on twenty-one, John knew he was dealing with a real pro. The marble lobby was sleek; fantastic portraits of celebrities and models covered the walls. Some he recognized, and others he didn't. He walked up to the receptionist and asked to speak to Alan Holden. She asked if he had an appointment. John took out his FBI credentials and said, "I just made one!" While the receptionist was making a call, he looked down at his PDA. It was five fifteen. She hung up the phone and said, "Mr. Holden is in a meeting. He wanted to know if you could make an appointment to see him next week." "Tell Mr. Holden that he is a person of interest in a homicide case, and I want to see him now." The receptionist relayed the message and told him to take a seat. John walked through the lobby looking at the photographs and magazines on the tables. John took off his jacket, and the receptionist couldn't help but notice his sheer size, the muscles bulging through his dress shirt, and the weapon in its holster on his left hip. She was just about to say something when Brenda Adams appeared and addressed him. "I take it from the gun you are carrying, you are Special Agent John Swenson." He nodded, "I am Mr. Holden's personal assistant. Will you follow me, please?" He nodded and followed the buxom blond bombshell down the hall to a corner office. "How much of this floor does Mr. Holden's company take up?" John asked. "The whole floor and the one above it." She walked him into the office and invited him to sit down. He did, and as he did, Alan Holden came walking in.

"What in God's name are you doing telling my receptionist that I am a person of interest in a homicide?" John turned in his seat then stood up. Holden stopped and jumped back as John's hulking frame cast a shadow over him. "Jesus Christ! Is the FBI breeding a new super race?" John didn't smile; he just looked Holden in the eyes and asked, "Mr. Holden, I presume?" He nodded and walked around his desk and sat down. He asked Brenda to stay, and she sat down next to John. "What can I do for you, Agent…" He looked at Brenda. "Swenson, sir. I'm sorry this is Special Agent John Swenson with the FBI." "Ah…thank you. Special Agent Swenson, on what grounds do you dare barge into my office and make such accusations?"

John handed him a piece of paper from his coat pocket. "Is this a copy of your business card, Mr. Holden?" He looked at the paper and said, "Yes, it is. How did you get it?" "It was in the bedroom of a young girl found murdered yesterday whose body was found at the Hollywood dam. Her name was Suzy Strom. Did you know her?" Holden looked closely at the business card. There was writing on what appeared to be a copy of the back of the card with an address. "I have no clients by that name, Special Agent Swenson." "I didn't ask you that, Mr. Holden. I asked if you know this young girl." "The name doesn't ring any bells with me." John reached into his jacket pocket again and took out a photograph and handed it to Alan. "Perhaps this will jog your memory." He handed him her most recent school picture. Alan took it from John's hand and looked at it very carefully. "She does look familiar, but I'm not sure from where." John sat up in the chair and asked, "Think hard, Mr. Holden. Think really hard."

He looked at the photo some more and said, "I recall seeing this little girl a few weeks ago at Zuma Beach. Yes, I remember. I saw her with her mother. She was a very cute girl, and I remember speaking to her mother about modeling. I gave her mother my card, but she had no interest. You said she has been found murdered?" John nodded. "Did you only give one card to the mother?" Alan got a thoughtful look on his face and said, "No. Her daughter was interested in modeling, and I gave her a card as well." John sat back and asked, "There's an address written in the dead girl's handwriting. Does the address mean anything to you?" He shook his head. "May I ask where you were between ten p.m. and two a.m. two nights ago?" Alan got a thoughtful look on his face. "Brenda? Do you have my calendar?" She pulled it up and handed it to him on her tablet. "I was with Holly Bachman, Agent Swenson. She had flown in from New York for a photo shoot with me for a new movie she is getting ready to release. She was with me for the last three days." "Where is she now?" "On a plane to New York. She has an engagement on the late night talk show circuit. Why do you ask?" "I would just like to verify your story with her."

Alan looked at him indignantly. "Are you accusing me of lying, Agent Swenson?" "No, sir. Your business card was found in the possession of a young girl who is now dead, the victim of a brutal homicide. That makes you a person of interest, and it's my job to investigate any leads that there might be in this case, and you are one of those leads. Have you seen this child since the time you first met her at Zuma Beach with her mother?" Alan shook his head. "Is there anyone other than Ms. Bachman who can verify your whereabouts for the last two days?" "Agent Swenson, Ms. Bachman will be back in LA in a few days. I am more than happy to make her available for you to speak with. However, I have a plane to catch in a few hours to be with my client in New York. Now unless you have some pressing information that proves that I have done something wrong, I must ask you to excuse me, so I can finish my business here and get to my client." John stood up and put on his jacket. "When will Ms. Bachman be back in Los Angeles?" "Um… it's Tuesday, so probably Friday." "Morning, afternoon, or night?" "Brenda?" Alan pointed to her, and she took her tablet and looked at the schedule. "Ms. Bachman will be back in LA Friday afternoon after three p.m." John thanked them for their time and asked Holden to make Ms. Bachman available for an interview at four p.m. on Friday. Alan looked on as John was leaving and asked, "Do I need my lawyer?" John never turned around as he answered, "Only if you have done something wrong, Mr. Holden, only if you have done something wrong."

John walked out to the elevator and went down to his truck. He got in and called Jim and said, "Meet me at Santiago's. I just had an interesting meeting with Alan Holden." "What time?" "Geez, Jim. Aren't you the one who always says it's five o'clock somewhere?" John said with a laugh. "You're goddamn right it is. I'm on my fuckin' way!" Jim hung up the phone, and John pulled out onto the Avenue of the Stars and headed for Santiago's.

"Ally…Ally…" The girl was out cold, and her kidnapper stood over her gently trying to wake her. She was stripped nude, and he was playing with her breasts as he called her name again. She began to rouse, and as she did she realized she was tied down. She started screaming, and her captor shoved her panties into her mouth. "Silence. You want to be a model? You are a gift to me from your to-be agent. He's used your body for his pleasure; now it's my turn. I'm here to help you realize my dream now, Ally…my dream." He stepped back out of the light and started snapping pictures of the girl. She struggled a bit, but her captor was easily able to instill fear in her. He kept taking shots of her as he moved across the small room and sat down on the edge of a dark table. "Ally…you and I are going to have fun. You're going to do everything I tell you to." Ally shook her head violently. He reached over to the table, which was obscured by darkness, and grabbed a pair of needle-nose pliers. He walked slowly over to the child saying, "Oh, yes you will. I promise you will."

He pulled her thighs apart and held her legs open with a steel rod with a block of wood on each end. He knelt down and began pinching the lips of her labia. She screamed through the gag. He ignored her cries but kept repeating to her, "You're going to do everything I tell you to. You're going to do everything I tell you to." He stood up and asked, "Are you going to cooperate?" She was crying as she slowly nodded her head. "That's great. We're going to have some real fun." He put the pliers down and stripped off his clothes. As he did, Ally watched with fear as he started to touch her all over. He released her hands and feet and took her panties out of her mouth. "There is no way you can please me with these in your mouth now is there?" She shook her head slowly. He pulled her head down and pushed himself forward toward her face.

John pulled into the lot at Santiago's, and Jim was already there. He walked in to receive a warm greeting from Javier. Jim was drinking a beer with a cigarette between his teeth when John sat down. Javier hobbled over to the table and handed John a glass of tonic water with a lime. "Jesus Christ, John. You fuckin' drink now, so put some gin or vodka in that." "I don't drink and drive, Jim. You know that." Jim shook his head, finishing off one beer and opening another. "What's the emergency?" John took a sip of his drink and said, "I just finished meeting with Mr. Holden." Jim shrugged and asked, "And?" "If he's a killer, he has one hell of a front going. His modeling and talent agency is real, and it's impressive." Jim coughed and started to laugh, "Simon Barstow was a legitimate businessman, too, John. Do you remember that fuckin' guy?"

John nodded. Jim laughed again and asked, "Want some bread or coffee cake?" John scowled. "Not funny, Jim." "It's funny. Are you kidding? That fucker was feeding his victims to the general public. He was a legitimate businessman; he just happened to be a serial killer." John frowned and took another drink of his beverage.

"Okay, you made your point. Holden is flying to New York tonight to meet up with one of his clients. I thought I would go visit his home." Jim laughed as he finished off his second beer and reached for the third. "Hey, the fucker is out of town. Get a secret warrant and search until your heart's content." "No warrants. I want to keep this under the radar." Jim got a serious look on his face and leaned in close to John and said, "The Eagle wants to take a look around." John didn't answer. "So ... what do you need from me?" Jim asked as he cracked open the beer. "I need you to check the flight schedule and make sure that Holden really is on a plane to New York." Jim laughed and nodded saying, "That's easy enough to do." John got up, thanked Javier, and left the bar. Jim called out for another beer and Javier said, "No more 'less you have driver." Jim put his jacket on and headed for the door. "Just what I fuckin' need, Javier. A responsible bar owner!" Nothing more was said as Jim walked out the door to his car. He radioed into HQ that he needed a trace on Holden's flight status and gave the information to his team. "I'm heading for home. Call me with all the details when you verify that Mr. Holden is on a plane." He hung up the phone and headed for the house he and Barbara had built in the Malibu hills.

Ally was breathing deeply and crying as her assailant got off her back. He walked back over to the table in the middle of the room and said, "Well, Ally, I have had a great time with you. I got some great shots. It's time for you to go." She was crying on the small twin bed in the room where she had just been raped and abused again. He grabbed her by the arm and dragged her over to the table and threw her face first onto it. He slid her around until her breasts fell through two holes in the top of the table, and he lashed her to the steel unit with leather belts. He took a whip and began whipping her back as she screamed uncontrollably. He flipped a switch on the table, and the motors came to life. "This is going to hurt." He flipped a lever, and she felt her breasts as they were being beaten by something hard. She screamed in agony and tried to thrash on the table as, one by one, the units turned. And as they did, they turned Ally's breasts into chopped meat. When the machine was done, he removed the restraints and flipped her onto her back. Blood and what had once been a beautiful young pair of breasts had been reduced to slivers of meaty flesh.

He tied her hands above her head with rope that was connected to the table, grabbed a funnel, and shoved it into Ally's mouth and down her throat. "Here is a little beverage for you before you go." He poured the contents from a bleach bottle into the funnel, and Ally gagged and strained, kicking her unrestrained feet in the air down onto the table until her legs went limp, and blood and liquid was running out an opening in her throat and side. "You did great!" the male voice said as he pulled the funnel from the young girl's throat. Her eyes were open as well as her mouth, neck, and throat. Ally was dead. He looked on at his prize and caressed her thighs before picking her up to take her to dump.

It was eight thirty p.m. when the Eagle arrived at Holden's home. He parked off the access road below the Getty Center, donned his mask and body armor, and moved through the darkness with night vision goggles. He approached the front of the home as a pair of headlights was coming up from behind him. He ducked into some foliage and watched as the vehicle passed. "There are no other homes on this street," he mumbled to himself then whispered, "probably kids making out." He worked his way to the front entrance and a wrought iron gate. He took out a tablet from his body armor, and in a matter of seconds, the gate was opening. There were no lights as he moved up the driveway. He had his countersurveillance gear on but was picking up no outside security. He looked around the premises. He saw a pool and tennis court off the main house and a couple of outbuildings. He moved his way to the front door of the home and was able to slip in after bypassing the simple home security system.

The Eagle moved from room to room in the house, but there was nothing out of the ordinary. He moved to the master bedroom. There was a double sliding glass door at the end of the room, and he saw that they opened into the back yard near the pool. He opened the slider and moved toward the outbuildings. The lights from the Getty Center were bright above him making it hard to see with his night vision on. He turned it off and put the glasses on top of his head. The furthest outbuilding was locked. It had an electronic lock. He pulled out his remote, and in a matter of seconds, the mechanism clicked, and the door opened. He moved inside the dark room and put his night vision goggles back on. As he started to look around, his nostrils were assaulted and his olfactory senses were overwhelmed by the smell of ammonia. He moved in the direction of the source of the odor. It took only seconds for him to see the remnants of human flesh and blood running down the sides of table. He moved around the room and saw the instruments of torture used.

He exited the building, took out his cell phone, and hit speed dial. "O'Brian!" "Where is Holden?" "Well, based on his itinerary, he is probably somewhere over the Rocky Mountains right now. Why?" There were a few moments of silence. "There will be another body tonight." Jim didn't respond. "Eagle out." He moved through the darkness to the second outbuilding, which had the same simple locking mechanism. When he looked through his night vision goggles at the room, he could see that it was a bedroom with personal items in it that the Eagle knew belonged to a killer. He made his way back to the house, but there was nothing in the house that indicated foul play.

When he got back to his truck, he took off the mask and called Jim back. Jim answered and asked, "What did the Eagle find?" "A recent murder scene. A killing done within minutes of the Eagle's arrival." "It's not Holden. He's long gone, brother!" "Run everything you can on this property. I'll do the same. Somehow I have to get to the next crime scene before the killer does." There was silence on the other end of the line. John asked, "Jim? Are you still there?" "Yea, John, yea… you're the fuckin' expert in this shit, John, not me. If you think you know where he's going to dump the body let me know, and I will get a team out there." John was shaking his head to himself. "I suspect I know where the dump will be, and I'm on my way. If the Eagle doesn't catch the killer dumping the body, we will have to stake out Holden's home in the hopes of catching this killer." The line went dead as John took off back to the 405 Freeway and the hopes of catching the killer. He knew where the killer liked to dump the bodies; he also knew he had to beat him there.

CHAPTER FOUR

"How could I forget?
You never fail to remind me."

Clive Montgomery arrived on scene for the new movie that Holly Bachman was shooting, which was a follow up to the current one she was promoting. Holly was in New York with Alan, and Holden instructed him to work out the final details on her quarters before shooting began. He was met by several producers of the movie and spent the better part of the late evening wrapping things up, so Alan wouldn't have to deal with the issues … and so he, himself, wouldn't get smacked around by Alan for not getting the job done. He had handed the producers his tablet and said, "So, you have the list of Ms. Bachman's demands in order to shoot your follow up film." Oscar Wilson sat looking at the .pdf file and looked up at Clive and asked, "She wants a double-wide three thousand square foot star wagon, an entertainment system, video game console, private chef, four personal assistants, a manicurist, a personal massage therapist, and a locked set so she won't be disturbed?" Wilson said this in a very monotone voice. Montgomery nodded. "On top of the fifteen million we are paying her, the royalty agreement, and the merchandising contracts?" Clive nodded. "Are you out of your damn minds? This is a movie that has ten major stars in it, all making less money than Ms. Bachman. I have personally had to beg and plead with the studio NOT to kill this project. We are already over budget by seven figures, and we haven't even shot one frame of footage." Wilson sat still just staring at Montgomery. There were a few tense moments of silence, and Wilson said, "Look...I've stuck my neck out as far as I am going to here. Need I remind you and your princess that I'm bankrolling the majority of this film? That we have no receipts from the first film yet to tell us if it is going to be a seller and if the audience is going to accept your teenage supermodel client as a serious actress? No! That's the answer to Ms. Bachman's demands. If we get a hit out of the first film, we will know it before cameras start rolling, and I will revisit these demands with you, but until then she will abide by her contract and be a star just like the rest of the cast. She needs to get over herself, and you and Holden need to handle your little princess before she blows her career out of the water before it ever gets started." Clive stood up and said, "Without these agreements, our client will not do the film." Oscar stood up and said, "She will do the movie, and she will follow her contract, or we will sue Holden, you, and Bachman. I'm finished with kiddy land; I'm going home."

Clive tried to yell something at Wilson as he walked away, but he simply waved a dismissive arm and walked out of sight. Clive pulled out his cell phone and called Alan. It was nearly three a.m. in New York when Alan groggily answered the phone. "I just finished the meeting with Wilson." Alan pulled himself up on his elbows in bed with the cell phone to his ear and asked, "So?" "The bottom line is no to the demands, and he has made it clear that if we don't produce Holly for filming he will sue." There were a few moments of silence on the phone, and Clive could hear a soft female voice on the other end of the line talking to Alan. Clive pulled the phone close to his mouth and asked, "Please tell me you're not fucking Holly?" "We will deal with Oscar when I get back to LA. They will give us what we want once the movie releases and Holly wows a skeptical audience." Clive wasn't deterred by the change in conversation. "Alan, are you fucking Holly?" "I need to get some sleep, Clive. I will speak to you tomorrow. Good night." The phone went dead, and Clive stood with the phone in his hand, looking up at the sky and whispered, "Jesus fucking Christ. He's going to end up in prison."

John turned his truck onto Lake Hollywood Drive just past midnight. He saw a sheriff's vehicle parked alongside the road and pulled up behind it. He got out and approached. The windows were fogged over, and the lights were off. John tapped on the window, and he heard fumbling and voices. The window rolled down, and the driver was fixing his pants as the young girl in the passenger seat was putting her blouse back on. The young deputy looked at John and asked, "WHAT?" in a rude and curt manner. John looked on at the two and asked, "How old are you, young lady?" "Don't say a word," the deputy told her. He moved to get out of the patrol SUV, but John pushed the door back against him. "Now, you listen to me, asshole. You just got yourself one count of assault on a sheriff's deputy." John pulled out his cell phone and his ID and flashed his badge at the deputy, all while calling Jim's cell phone. "You two stay right where you are. Don't move a muscle," John said as he raised the phone to his ear.

"WHAT…WHAT…WHAT?" The look on the deputy's face said it all. He could tell from the sound of the screaming on the other end of Special Agent Swenson's phone that he had called Sheriff Jim O'Brian. "Sorry to bother you, Jim, but I'm out here at Lake Hollywood and came across one of your deputy's vehicles. I thought I would stop and see if there had been anything unusual. Instead, I'm standing here in front of your man's vehicle where he was getting a blow job from an underage girl." There were a few moments of silence, and John hung up the phone. "Sheriff O'Brian will be right along. Both of you step out of the vehicle, please." The deputy stepped out while John walked around to make sure the girl didn't bolt. The headlights on his truck were shining at the back of the SUV, and he brought the two to the back for a better look. The girl couldn't have been fifteen. The deputy motioned to say something, and John lifted his hand and gestured with his fingers for him to shut up. There were a few more moments of silence before Jim pulled up on scene. Jim looked the two over then pulled a radio off his belt and called for another unit. He ordered the young deputy to surrender his weapon, and John placed him under arrest. Jim handcuffed the girl, who was somber but in no way surprised.

"What's your name?" Jim asked. "What do you want it to be?" Jim sighed and shrugged his shoulders. "I want it to be your real name; I'm only going to ask one more time before I print you here and now." "Jessica…Jessica Holmes." "How long have you been hooking?" "Um…I don't know. Three or four years." "Where do you live?" "Wherever there's a bed." Jim left Jessica with John and walked his deputy to his car as another sheriff's cruiser pulled up. "How old are you?" John asked. "Sixteen." "Where are your parents?" "The last time I saw my mother she was being cremated after a drug overdose. As for my father, the last time I saw him he was grunting and sweating over me as he raped me and beat me up." John took her arm and walked her back to Jim's car and put her in the back seat. "Are you going to read me my rights?" "Yea, in a minute. I need to speak to the sheriff." John closed the back door to the car and walked over to Jim standing in the middle of the road smoking a cigarette.

"She says she's sixteen." Jim took a deep hit off the smoke and said, "I don't care if she's forty; my deputy is under arrest for multiple violations of law and his duty as a peace officer. I just sent him back to the station with my deputies. What are you going to do with her?" "I'm releasing her to your custody, Jim. I put her in your car." "You know it's only an overnight stay in the jail. She will be out by morning." "You can call social services and child protective services for her," John said staring off in the direction of the lake. "Yea…I will take care of it." Just then a call came over Jim's radio to all units — a body had been found near Hollywood Lake Park. The two men ran for their vehicles and headed in the direction of the park. They didn't need directions; the spinning lights of two LAPD cruisers lit up the area with their spot lights.

John parked and jumped out, and he and Jim met up on the top of a knoll overlooking the city. There was a nude female body laid on her back in a display of brutality. Her breasts were gone, and her body was badly beaten. John looked around and asked, "Who was here first?" Two LAPD officers walked over to him and said they arrived on scene less than five minutes prior. "How did you find the body?" John asked, looking at the girl's bloody carcass. "We received a dispatch from 911 that there was a body in the park. We got here, and this is what we found." John called for his team and then walked over to look at the girl's body. She had been tortured. Jim walked up behind him and said, "If it hadn't been for my asshole deputy, you might have gotten here before the killer." John nodded, and as he did he heard screaming coming from the back of Jim's car. It was Jessica. John hadn't thought about it when they pulled up on scene, and Jim had parked his car to the side, and the passenger window faced the crime scene. Jim shook his head and said, "Hold on. Let me go move the kid before she splits a gut." Jim walked down the knoll and opened the car door. Jessica had had her head against the window of the car, and there was spit and fog from her screaming. Jim opened the door, and she bolted out of the car and up the knoll toward the body. She was screaming something, but he couldn't make it out.

John saw and heard her and turned just as she reached the scene. He grabbed her as she fell to her knees calling out a name and trying to move her hands that were cuffed behind her back. Jim ran to the top of the hill, and when he got there, he heard Jessica saying, "Ally, Ally…oh my God. Ally!" John and Jim both looked at each other. Once they got Jessica back on her feet, they walked her away from the body. John looked down at the teary face of the girl and asked, "How do you know her?" She was hyperventilating as she tried to speak through tears and hard breaths. "She's my friend. She's my friend." There was a bench near the lake, and John and Jim walked her over to it and sat her down. "What's her name?" Jim asked calmly. "Ally…Ally Morrison." Jim pulled out his midi recorder, and John walked back to his truck to grab his tablet.

The two men began to question Jessica. John asked, "You said she's your friend. Is she a prostitute?" She shook her head. "Is she someone you went to school with?" She shook her head once more. "Then, how do you know her?" "She's a missionary with the Hollywood mission. I met her about a year ago. She had been on the streets, too, but had found religion and was trying to guide me to her cause." John looked on as the coroner's van pulled up with Jade and her team. She saw John and Jim and walked over to them. She didn't see Jessica and said, "Is it me or are you two getting better and better at finding your way to these scenes as they happen?" She moved to face John and saw Jessica. "I'm sorry, gentlemen. Do we have a witness?" John shook his head. "This young lady knows the victim."

Jade stepped back and moved out of sight. Jim sat down next to Jessica and removed the handcuffs. She saw the silver flash from the cigarette pack in his left top pocket. "Can I have a cigarette?" Jim pulled out the pack, lit the smoke, and handed it to her then lit his own. Jessica was trembling as she took a hit off the cigarette. She drew a deep breath off the smoke and released it from her lungs into the night sky. "You said she used to be on the streets, so was she a prostitute?" Jim asked. She took another hit and said, "She was way worse than me according to what she called her 'testimony.' She was into drugs, prostitution, and porn. You name it. I haven't seen her for a few weeks. I thought maybe she had lapsed in her faith or was in rehab." Jim sat looking at the city from the bench then looked over at Ally's body and back at Jessica.

"You said she was a missionary. What church?" She took another drag of the cigarette and said, "I'm not sure about the denomination, but they run a mission off Hollywood and Vine. I ate there with her once or twice, but I had no interest in the religion stuff she was into." Jim asked, "Can you remember exactly when the last time you saw her was? "Um…like I said…it's been a few weeks." She had a thoughtful look on her face then said, "Actually, it was three nights ago. She was dressed in a school girl's outfit. I remember she looked really slutty, and I asked if she was back on the streets. She told me that she was doing a play with a group of actors, and she was on her way to rehearsal. I don't know what kind of play she was in. If it was religious, it was twisted." "What makes you say that?" Jim asked. "Because she was braless in a tight low cut top and a short skirt without panties. She had tits on parade, and I even commented that it must be one hell of a play. She told me that she had some promising new contact that was going to help her become a star."

Jim looked at her for a long time as John was typing on his tablet. "Did she mention anything about the contact or the person that was going to help her?" "No…I saw her walk to the corner of Hollywood and Vine not far from the mission and then on down Hollywood Boulevard. Then I lost sight of her." "Do you know how old she was?" Jim asked. "My age. She might have been a little younger. You would never have known it when you saw her made up though. She was really pretty." Jim walked her back to one of his patrol units and told them to take her downtown but not to book her. He told them to call child protective services but not to have her removed from the building until he was able to speak with everyone. He turned to leave when she asked, "That could have been me, huh?" Jim didn't miss a beat. He said, "You're goddamn right it could have been and could still be unless you get your shit together. I will speak to you at my office in a few hours."

Jim walked back up the knoll. John had left him with Jessica and was with Jade when he asked, "Are you two talking about your affair or the case?" John frowned as did Jade. "This is not the time for jokes, Jim. John was asking me to get an autopsy and time of death on this kid." Jim looked on and said, "Jessica is being taken downtown, and child protective services is coming. I told my people she is not to leave the building until I have spoken with her some more." John nodded, and Jade walked back up to the body. Jim took out a cigarette and asked, "So, are you going to tell me what's going on between you and Jade?" "Nothing, Jim. You know that." "Then what's going on between Sara and Jade?" John shook his head as he walked back toward his truck.

"Listen, John, I've been down this road with Barbara. If something is going on between Jade and Sara and you're not involved, you're headed down a bad road, my friend." John kept walking as he answered, "We are all friends, Jim. That's all. And based on this killing, Holden has an airtight alibi. Whoever killed this kid has access to Holden's home and outbuildings." Jim was trying to keep up with John who was walking at a brisk pace. "Well, then we better investigate the people who work for him, and we better get Holden in for questioning as soon as he's back in town. I'm not buying that Holden knows nothing about this. Remember the Barstow case?" John nodded as he got into his truck and said, "How could I forget? You never fail to remind me."

Hillary Sums' article on the Hollywood Killer had been on the front page of every tabloid magazine in Los Angeles and around the world. She and her partner, Terry Brady, had been freelance writers in the entertainment industry for years. They had recently branched out into more sophisticated journalistic writing in the hopes of grabbing a larger market share for their work and audience. Hillary's most recent article on the murder of Suzy Strom had garnered some harsh criticism from not just the general public but also those in her inner circle. She had been receiving death threats because of her article sensationalizing the child's killing as one of 'passion and desperation.'

"Suzy Strom, while the victim, was known to her friends as a spoiled brat and a tramp. A friend speaking on the condition of anonymity said that Suzy felt she was immune to the rules that society placed on others because her father is a high-ranking Los Angeles Police Detective. 'She always had her nose in the air about other people.

If you ask me, she invited the killer into her life, and she got what she deserved.' While Ms. Strom's death is tragic, because of her background and the people she associated with, she is dead for one reason and one reason only, EGO!"

Hillary was just getting ready to leave her office on Santa Monica Boulevard when Terry walked in. "Don't you think that your story telling on the Strom murder is just a bit over the top?" Terry asked with a disapproving look on her face. "This coming from the woman who taught me everything there is to know about exploiting a situation to sell a story." Hillary stood up and was packing her laptop into her bag. "Hill, I love you. We found this poor kid's body near our home. You're plastering unflattering stories that you and I know are fabricated. The Strom girl was a good kid." "How the hell would you know? You dare accuse me of fabricating witnesses?" She was shoving the rest of her stuff into her laptop case as Terry approached. She put her hand on Hillary's shoulder and said, "I love you. Please, please don't keep doing this. You have no sources. I've checked the story out. The Strom girl's dead because a sicko ended her life. You're not the only one getting death threats. We're a couple, and people know that. I'm getting them, too. You're on this killer's radar and on her father's. Be careful." Hillary grabbed her bag and laptop case and swung it over her shoulder. "Don't be so damned dramatic. We've had death threats before. There's no reason to take these any more serious than any others. I'm doing my job. I'm reporting the news. Maybe it's sensationalized, but, hey, that's what sells papers. Isn't that what you told me?" Terry just turned and walked out of the office with Hillary hot on her heels. Not to respond but to leave. "Where are you going in such a hurry?" Terry asked. "I got a lead on the hooker, Ally Morrison. I need to follow up on it. It will make great fodder for the next Hollywood Killer segment I'm writing." She bolted into an open elevator and out of sight.

It was half past eight p.m. as Hillary made her way across the parking structure to her Mercedes convertible. She popped the trunk as she approached and threw her bags into it. She was about to enter her vehicle when a dark figure appeared near the pillar she was parked in front of. "So, you like making up sick and twisted stories about innocent children?" a male voice said from the darkness. She had no response; she was paralyzed with fear. She turned to run, but the man moved and grabbed her by the back of the neck and placed a handkerchief over her face as he pulled her over to the passenger side of her car. He put her in the front seat then got in the driver seat and drove the car out of the lot onto Santa Monica Boulevard.

John had learned Alan Holden's itinerary and was waiting for him at LAX when his plane landed. Holden emerged from the private jet area of LAX with a young woman. Holden saw John right away and said, "This is harassment, Special Agent Swenson!" "You must be Holly Bachman?" John asked. Holly nodded. "This is not harassment, Mr. Holden. It is the follow up to our previous conversation as promised. If you will both come with me please." Holden got pissed and started yelling at John while at the same time dialing his cell phone. "I'll be dammed if I'm going to have the FBI pushing me around. I have answered your questions. My client has rights as do I, and I want my lawyer present when we talk to you." John stood silent while Holden spoke to his attorney on the phone. When he hung up, Holden said, "I don't have to do shit for you, Agent Swenson, neither does my client."

John walked toward the two slowly. He had one hand on his face rubbing under his chin as he spoke in a soft gentle tone. "No...Mr. Holden, you and Ms. Bachman don't have to speak to me right now. You two can get in your car and drive home." Holden started throwing their bags into the trunk of his car as John continued. "However, if you refuse to cooperate with my investigation, you will force me to get a subpoena for you and your client. The subpoena will state that it is for the FBI's investigation into the Hollywood Killer, and it will be PUBLIC RECORD. You think the media hounds you and your client now? Well, I don't think I have to tell you what type of media circus that will bring on. And since you have told me you know nothing of these killings, the fact that the FBI has to subpoena you and Ms. Bachman to answer some really, really simple questions will look like a man and his client with something to hide." John smiled at Holly who was standing frozen. Staring up at the giant man, she asked, "What is this all about, Alan?"

He was standing still, staring into John's eyes. He could see from John's expression that he could make a hell of this situation quickly. John started to walk away while pulling his cell phone from his hip. He dialed a number and made sure he was in earshot of Holden and Bachman as he made the call. "This is Special Agent John Swenson. Put in requests for two subpoenas for Alan Holden and Holly Bachman as persons of interest in the Hollywood Killer case. I need them ASAP, so push them through with Judge Erickson. She is always willing to accommodate me." There were a few moments of silence as the person on the other end of the phone was speaking. He drew a deep breath in and responded, "No...these subpoenas can be public record...in fact, why don't you make sure the media outlets know about the orders once they have been granted."

"Okay…OKAY! Where the hell do you want to talk to me and my client?" John told the person on the other end of the line to hold. "My office at the federal building." Holden was clearly annoyed and asked, "When?" John looked down at his watch; it was eight thirty. "Now! You and Ms. Bachman can follow me back to my office, or I can drive you." "I want my lawyer there," Holden said with his hands on his hips. "Fine. I want you two in my office now." John got into his truck as Holden and Bachman got into his car. John could see Holden on the phone behind him. John called Jim. "Yea!" "I have Holden and Bachman following me back to my office for questioning. Care to join me?" Jim let out a deep belly laugh in response. "Oh, hell yea…I wouldn't miss this for the world. When?" "Now." "Shit, asshole. Thanks for the advance notice…I'm on my way. Don't start without me." "I won't. He called his lawyer." Jim laughed. "Big fuckin' surprise. It's always the guilty ones who want their lawyers there. I'm on my way." Jim hung up the line and yelled out into the outer office, "I'm on my way to the federal building. Call my cell if you need me." He put on his suit coat as he headed for the door.

Hillary was flat on her back on a piece of plywood, which was elevated by stacked cinderblocks, with a second board running the length of her body and three concrete cinderblocks stacked on top of her chest. Gasping, she cried out, "Please… please. I'm sorry." "You're sorry? You're sorry? You're goddamn right you're sorry." The man paced in front of the blocks on her chest. "You like to write lies and sensationalize the death and torture of children. YOU SHOULD BE GODDAMNED SORRY!" Her captor placed another block on her chest, and she heaved a heavy breath under the weight. Her voice was merely a whisper as the air was being squeezed out of her. "I'll retract…I'll retract all of it." Her captor sat down on a steel folding chair next to her head and looked into her eyes. "Do you know what it is that I'm doing to you?" She slowly shook her head as her breathing became more and more labored under the weight of the block. "It's called 'pressing.' It's a medieval form of torture, and it is very effective." He whispered into her left ear, "It was used to get confessions out of witches. You are nothing but a fuckin' witch. How do you like the pressure? Feel good, you bitch?"

The plywood underneath her started to crack as her torturer placed yet another block on top of her chest. Her respiration was becoming erratic, and she was trying to scream from the pain, but she couldn't take in enough air. Her head was bobbing from side to side as if she were looking for an exit. Her arms were pinned and tears were running down her face as the plywood beneath her cracked again. "You don't deserve to live...I don't want a retraction. The damage has been done. You ruined my life. You ruined a lot of people's lives. You have no remorse. It was all a game to you. When the board beneath you breaks, all of this weight is going to come down on your chest breaking your ribs and collapsing your lungs. It will be the agonizing death you deserve." "Please," she whispered with little breath left in her lungs, "mercy." "You used my child as a tabloid figure, and you want mercy? No, Ms. Sums. No mercy. You don't deserve mercy. I will tell you before you die that I will find the animal that raped and mutilated my little girl and much worse will happen to him. You are going to die...I just want to watch you suffer."

Randy Strom lifted two cinderblocks and laid them on Hillary Sums' chest. She drew a deep breath and let out a howl of anguish as the plywood she was laying on split in two, sending her body and the weight down onto the concrete floor of the building she had been taken to. Randy walked around to look her in her dying eyes...a trickle of blood was dripping out of the corner of her mouth. Her pupils were dilating when Randy spoke the last words she would ever hear. "Next, I will deal with your girlfriend, Ms. Brady." Strom walked out of the room leaving Hillary's dead body under the stacked blocks. The building was under construction in downtown Los Angeles. He talked to himself as he got on the exterior crane elevator to the high rise and said, "The contractor will find your body, and you're in my jurisdiction, so you will be my homicide case. Now to get Ms. Brady and...'press' her for information." He pressed the button, and the elevator began its descent through the LA darkness.

CHAPTER FIVE

"Are you going to get to the bottom of what you want from this asshole, or are you going to dance with him all night?"

Jim was sitting with John, Holden, and Bachman in an interrogation room. He looked down at his watch; it was half past nine, and John was questioning Holden about everything under the sun. Jim's patience was growing thin. "Are you going to get to the bottom of what you want from this asshole, or are you going to dance with him all night?" asked Jim. John shot him a disapproving look, but Jim sat stoic. Holden's lawyer hadn't shown up yet, and he was refusing to cooperate. The phone in the interrogation room buzzed, and John answered it. "Mr. Holden's counsel is here, Agent Swenson." "Male or female?" "Male." "Clear him and send him up." John sat staring at Holden who was staring at Holly. The interrogation room was silent until there was a knock on the door. John opened it to see Howard Cohen standing before him.

Howard stepped back, and John stepped forward into the hall. "Oh, come on, Howard. Don't tell me that Holden is your client?" He nodded and asked to be let into the room. John opened the door, and the two men entered. Alan reached out for Howard, but Howard kept his distance with a quick handshake. "John. Jim. What's the situation?" Howard could feel the air come out of Holden when he addressed the men by their first names. "You know these two?" Howard nodded. "Howard, what the hell? You know these two cops?" "Don't say another word, Alan, or you, Ms.

Bachman." "Howard, I think you might have a conflict here," John said looking on at Holden. "What are the charges, Agent Swenson?" John looked Howard in the eye and said, "There are no charges at this time, Howard. Mr. Holden and Ms. Bachman are persons of interest in a homicide. All I am seeking are answers regarding your client's whereabouts for the past three days." Howard looked at Alan and Holly and then asked John, "May I have a moment to confer with my clients?" John nodded, and he and Jim stood up and walked out of the room.

"What a crock of shit. Is Howard Cohen the only goddamn lawyer in Los Angeles?" Jim asked angrily. "If you have the money, yes Jim." They both were silent when Howard came out and invited them back into the room. "Mr. Holden and Ms. Bachman are invoking their Fifth Amendment rights," Howard said in a sad tone. Jim piped up and said, "That's fine for Mr. Holden, but Ms. Bachman is a minor. Where are her parents?" "Ms Bachman is a ward of the state, Sheriff. Mr. Holden is her guardian." "Oh, bullshit! Fuck this, John. Let's get a *guardian ad litem* assigned for the kid and get what we need that way." John looked at Howard and asked, "Is that the road I need to go down to get answers, Howard? I can have one assigned by a judge and in this room in a half hour. Do you want to go down that road?" Howard frowned, and Alan yelled, "What the hell is he talking about Howard? I've been caring for Holly for years." "Alan, Holly is still a minor, and since she has no parents to stand for her, and because the FBI and the sheriff's department are seeking answers from the two of you, you have a conflict as do I. She will need her own attorney, which is what Sheriff O'Brian is asking for and Agent Swenson is talking about doing."

Holden was visibly nervous, and John saw it right away. "What if we agree to answer their questions and waive our rights?" "You can do that, Alan, but Holly can't. I could be sued by you or her for malpractice if I didn't accept the fact that Sheriff O'Brian is right. You two need separate counsel, and the FBI has also pointed this out to me. I'm sorry." Howard looked at John and said, "Make the call. It's the right thing to do." John got the judge on the phone. Within ten minutes, there was an attorney from child protective services in the room with them, who advised Holly to remain silent and asked John to charge his client or release her. John released Holly, who was crying and screaming as she was taken out of the room. "I'm Holly Bachman; I'm a superstar. You can't take me away from my agent and friend." They pulled her out of the room, leaving Jim, John, Howard, and Alan alone. John said, "She's going to talk to me, Mr. Holden, and you can't see her. Now, do you want to answer my questions, or do we have to push this situation even farther?" Holden put his head down and shook it slowly as Howard rose from the table. "Well, Agent Swenson, charge my client or release him." John stood up and said, "Have it your way, Howard. Mr. Holden is free to go. I will get a subpoena for him right away, and if he won't talk to me, then I will send what evidence we have to the U.S. attorney and request that a grand jury be seated. One way or another, Mr. Holden, you are going to talk to me."

Holden was walking out of the interrogation room on the sixth floor of the federal building when John heard him ask Howard, "Is this going to be made public?" Howard nodded as they walked into the elevator. Jim looked at John and asked, "What does the Eagle know that I don't?" John shook his head and said, "It's not admissible in court, and the Eagle won't grab him until he knows for sure he's the bad guy." Jim took a cigarette out of his top left pocket and put it in his mouth. He started chomping on it and asked, "Since when does the Iron fuckin' Eagle give a rat's ass about illegal searches?" John's shoulders dropped, "He doesn't, but he just doesn't go around killing random people, Jim. You know that. Do I think that Holden's a bad man? You bet your ass I do. I just don't know how bad. I don't think he's the Hollywood Killer, but I have a feeling he knows who is." "Well, you better get this bizarre thinking worked out John because if you don't another kid is going to end up dead."

The words had no sooner left his mouth when Jim's cell phone rang. "WHAT?" John watched Jim's facial expressions until he hung up the phone. "Well?" John asked. "Well..." Jim pulled back his shoulders, "We have a homicide at a new high rise condo complex at the corner of South Figueroa and West Fourth Street. That was my team leader. He said we will want to be on scene for this one." John shrugged and asked why. "Because the victim is Hillary Sums." The two men headed for the elevator and the crime scene.

Sara walked through the front door of the house after nearly two days of grueling nonstop work. It was just nine thirty, and she looked around for any sign of her husband. She called John's cell, and he answered. "Hey, sweetheart. I just got home. Are you going to be home soon?" John was driving down the 110 Freeway headed for Fourth Street. "I'm sorry, Sara. I'm en route to a crime scene. It's going to be a late night." There was a moment of silence, and Sara said, "I understand, honey. We just haven't seen each other in nearly a week." "I know...there's a lot going on, Sara. I promise I will get home as soon as I can." There were a few I love yous, and Sara hung up. She walked out onto the deck off the living room and listened to the surf crashing on the beach.

She heard a familiar voice behind her and turned to see Jade Morgan standing in the hall between the front door and the living room in a robe. Sara smiled and invited her in. "Let me guess. You came for a swim in our pool because it's bigger?" Jade laughed, "Yea. It's been a tough week, and you guys have a much better view than I do, not that I'm complaining." Sara laughed and offered Jade a drink. They sat down on the couch and talked about their days. Jade took off her robe and walked nude across the living room out onto the deck and dove into the pool. Sara undressed and followed her, and the two swam for a few minutes before stopping and jumping into the Jacuzzi with their drinks to continue their conversation.

"So, I've heard Jim accused us of having a threesome, and that you and I are having an affair," Jade said. Sara had just taken a drink of her beverage and choked on it a bit. "You're kidding?" "Nope...Jim seems convinced that we're doing freaky things." Sara sat her drink on the edge of the Jacuzzi and laughed. "I will set him straight." Jade laughed. "Why bother? Let him think what he likes. We know the truth." Sara heard the doorbell ring as Jade finished her comment and waited to see who was calling. One of her personal assistants walked in the direction of the front door. "I will give you two guesses on who that is at this hour, but I bet you I will get it in one," Sara said to Jade as she sipped her drink.

They both saw Barbara O'Brian walk into the living room in her robe. Sara called out to her, and she walked out onto the back patio. "Let me guess...Jim is off on an adventure with John?" "I'm bored, and I knew you were supposed to be off tonight, so I thought I would drop by. Is it okay?" Sara and Jade both laughed. Sara stood up and walked out of the Jacuzzi and asked, "Scotch on the rocks?" Barbara smiled and nodded, taking off her robe and walking nude out to the Jacuzzi to join Jade in the water. Sara returned with the drink, sat back down in the warm water, and asked Barbara, "Did you know that Jim thinks that we — Jade, John, and I — are playing hanky-panky?" Barbara started laughing. "Yes... Jim has voiced his own concern about it to me." Jade asked, taking a sip of her drink, "What do you tell him?" "That it's none of his damn business and to worry about taking care of me!" Sara frowned. "Jade wants to let him spin on it. I think we should tell him that we are just friends, and we also happen to be nudists."

Barbara laughed, sipping her scotch. "Oh, no. You can't tell him that. It will take the fantasy out of it for him. I know that when he's fucking me he's thinking about you two, and I'm just fine with that. Let him have his little fantasy. We all know where we stand. Don't take the great sex away from me." There was a round of laughter until Jade heard her phone ringing in the pocket of her robe. She jumped out of the hot water and grabbed the robe and the phone.

"Jade Morgan." There were a few moments of silence before Jade spoke. "It's my night off for God's sake. David is on duty. He is my deputy medical examiner. He knows how to work a crime scene." There were a few more moments of silence, and then Jade said, "David…I know that you have your moments being ill at ease on a scene, but with John and Jim there as well, you will be fine. Write up the report. I will do the autopsy in the morning." There were a few more moments of silence, and Jade's expression changed. "Hi John. So you are on scene with David? I told him he can handle this. It's my night off … the first in a week. I'm with Barb and Sara. Can't I review the reports in the morning? I promise I'll do an autopsy first thing." Sara and Barbara were looking at each other, and Sara said to Barbara under her breath, "I'm a doctor, and I run an ER. I see my fair share of gore, but I could never do what Jade does for a living." Barbara nodded as Jade continued. "So you are okay with working the scene with Dave? Thank you, John. I will take care of things in the morning. Is the deceased anyone I know?" There were a few more moments of silence, and Jade gasped. "Jesus Christ…you're kidding? Oh, that's going to make the late news unless you're going to hold it back." Jade held the phone tight, and the two girls could see that something big was happening.

She hung up the phone and looked at the girls in the Jacuzzi. Sara looked at her and asked, "Jade, are you okay?" She shook her head slowly. "That was John. He and Jim are on a crime scene, and the victim is Hillary Sums." There was silence until Barbara piped up as Jade was settling back down into the water. "Well, if the bitch was murdered, she had it coming. Jim and I have talked a lot about her. She exploits terrible situations and sensationalizes them for her own gain. I guess she finally crossed the wrong person." Jade took a sip of her drink and said, "Whoever killed her pressed her to death." There was silence in the water. Barbara stood up and said, "I don't know about you two, but I'm hungry. Sara, can we ask your assistant to whip us up a little meal?" Sara nodded as they all stepped out of the water and onto the deck.

Jim was standing next to David Markham, Jade's deputy medical examiner, while John was examining the scene. Hillary Sums' body lay fully clothed and crushed under several hundred pounds of brick. "Who found her?" "A security guard walking patrol on the structure about an hour ago," Jim said, looking down at the squashed woman. David was ordering his CSI team in as John and Jim's teams were finishing up their crime scene analysis. "Well, I think we all know what the cause of death was." Jim said half laughing. John stood up and said, "We will have to wait for the autopsy. Jade promised she will do it first thing in the morning." Jim couldn't hold back and started laughing as Randy Strom walked toward them. "Oh, cut the shit, John. She looks like road kill, and the bitch got the guts crushed out of her."

Randy walked up and asked what they had. John looked over at him and asked, "Are you just arriving on scene?" He nodded. "Well, take a look for yourself. Someone decided to press her to death." Randy knelt down near Hillary's head and asked John, "Do you think it's the work of the Hollywood Killer?" Randy stood up, looking at John as he answered. "I hope the hell not, Randy. I hope the hell not." Jim looked at John and Randy for several seconds then chimed in. "This is not the work of the Hollywood Killer; this was personal. Whoever killed Ms. Sums wasn't trying to do anything more than torture and kill her. She's a hot chick; she's fully dressed, and her midsection is crushed. Nope…whoever killed Ms. Sums, here, had an axe to grind with her, and it wasn't the Hollywood Killer."

John handed Randy a pair of gloves, which he took and put on. "This is your jurisdiction, Randy. What do you want to do?" Randy knelt back down and flipped her hair and looked at the blocks that had crushed her to death. "It's my crime scene. My people will work it up." John walked over and helped David with the gurney then worked with David's team to move one block at a time and numbered them as evidence. Randy looked on and asked, "John, I told you it's my crime scene. I will deal with it!" John was effortlessly moving block after block as he spoke. "She's a national celebrity, Randy. It will only be your scene for another few seconds, then I'm going to get the call to take over. You know that, and I know that." No sooner had John said it when his cell phone rang with those exact orders.

Once Hillary was in a body bag and Dave was taking her to the elevator to go down to the van, John asked Randy, "Where were you when you got the call to come to this scene?" "Um…some of Suzy's friends were holding a vigil for her. Amy and I were there when the call came in." John stepped back and asked, "When is her funeral?" Randy's eyes got red and his voice was low. "Tomorrow morning at ten at our Sisters of the Holy Cross on Euclid." John said, "I will be there." Jim nodded and told him that he would be there as well. Randy thanked them, and John said, "Well… there's nothing more to see here. I will get the case report from those on scene and put a couple of my people on this homicide."

Randy looked on as John and Jim walked to the elevator that ran along the side of the high rise. Jim said, "I hate the steel cages they use for elevators on these tower cranes. I always feel like I'm falling." John nodded as they closed the steel cage, and the elevator began to lower. Jim looked at John, who had a deep look of concentration on his face. "You don't think we need to look too far for the killer here, do you?" Jim was taking out a cigarette as he asked the question. John shook his head. Jim put the smoke in his mouth and lit it while the elevator was still going down. "Well, you have a motive. The bitch did just what I said she would do when we were with them at Lake Hollywood." John nodded; Jim took a drag off the cigarette and asked, "Are you going to talk to Randy about it?" "Yea…after the funeral…I will give him a little time." "You think he's searching for the killer?" John looked Jim in the eye and asked, "Wouldn't you be?" Jim coughed, blowing the smoke out of his nose as they exited the elevator on the ground. "That was a stupid fuckin' question. I'm sorry, John. It was a stupid mother fuckin' question."

Jim arrived back at his office a little before midnight. Jessica was asleep on the sofa with one of his deputies standing guard outside the room. "Has she said anything more to you?" The deputy shook his head. "What about social services? Where is the case worker?" The officer adjusted his shirt and gun belt and said, "I'm not sure, Sheriff. There was someone here for a little while with her. The gal from social services told me that Ms. Holmes is an emancipated minor and out of their jurisdiction." Jim looked at the sleeping girl on his couch and said, "So, I have a kid who's an adult in the eyes of the law?" The deputy nodded, and Jim waved him off.

He walked in quietly as not to wake her. He moved over to the stool by the window where he kept his cigarettes and opened the window and flipped his Zippo open to light the smoke. He snapped it shut, but Jessica didn't move. It was half past midnight, and he took one of the penal code books that was sitting next to his desk, held it high, and dropped it. The book came slamming down, rattling his desk lamp, and jolting the sleeping girl. She sat straight up, looking at him. "So, you're a fuckin' emancipated minor?" She rubbed her eyes and asked, "How do you know that?" He took a hit off the cigarette and blew the smoke out the window. "Because that's what child protective services told me. What the hell's your deal, kid? Who the hell are you, and what are you doing on the street?" "It's where I live and have lived for the better part of five years. I make a living sucking the cocks of cops as well as others. I give them head, or let them do what they want to me, and in exchange I get protection and a few bucks."

Jim stubbed out the smoke in the ashtray and sat down at his desk. "Protection from what?" "Not just what but who, so I don't end up like Ally and some of the other girls that have died recently. And I don't have to have a pimp pressing me on the street." Jim spread his arms wide in a yawn. "I hate to break it to you, kiddo, but from what you just told me, the cops are your pimps. And there is no sense in getting you to name names and departments of officers, is there?" She slowly shook her head and asked, "Ally was killed by that serial killer...the Hollywood Killer, wasn't she?" Jim nodded, saying, "Right now it looks that way. You sure you didn't see her talking to anyone out of the ordinary before she was found?" She stretched out her arms and arched her back. She was slim and fit. Her skin was smooth, and her breasts were showing through the light white shirt she was wearing.

Jessica saw the way Jim was looking at her. She stood up and asked, "How about I give you a freebie, Sheriff? You look like a man with one stuck in the chamber." He laughed as he got up and walked over to the window for another cigarette." She asked if she could have one, so Jim grabbed the pack and told her to follow him. They went downstairs and out the front door of his building and sat down together on one of the benches in front of the station. He handed her a cigarette and lit it for her then one for himself.

"That line works for you a lot, doesn't it?" She took a drag off the cigarette and smiled. "It has to, Sheriff. I don't have a home to go to when the day is done." He took a hit off his smoke and looked her up and down. Her long brown hair was clean and groomed; her makeup was well done. She had beautiful facial features, and her deep brown eyes were compelling, almost beckoning. "If I didn't know your age I would guess you to be in your early twenties. That's probably why you're still alive." Her facial expression changed, and he asked again, "You did see Ally talking to someone, didn't you?" She took a hit off the cigarette and said, "Ally and I talked to all kinds of people. If you want me to say that I saw her talking to her killer, I can tell you that I don't think I saw that." Jim took in the night air with his arms spread on the back of the bench. "Where are you going to sleep tonight?" She shrugged, stubbing out the smoke in the concrete ashtray next to the bench. "It's early. Now that you have no reason to hold me if you would be kind enough to give me a ride back to the boulevard I'm sure I can find a john to sleep under tonight." Jim stood up and told her to follow him. They walked back into the building and up the stairs to his office. He grabbed his coat and said, "Come with me." Jessica didn't hesitate. She followed Jim down to his car, got in the passenger seat, and waited.

Jim was standing in front of the car talking with two men in sheriff's uniforms, then he walked over, got into the driver's side, and started the car. "Where are we going?" she asked in a casual manner. "You will stay with me and my wife tonight." She smiled and put her hand on his crotch. "You want me to give you head as you drive?" Jim sighed and lifted her hand and put it back on her lap. "No...I want you off the streets tonight. I want you to talk with Special Agent John Swenson of the FBI tomorrow. We are going to show you some pictures, and you're going to tell us if you know the people in them." She laughed a little under her breath, looking out the window as Jim turned the car onto PCH. "Well, this is a first for me. I get a bed, and I don't have to put out." Jim didn't look at her when he answered. "I want you alive in the morning, and I'm not convinced that if I left you on the street that you will be. I think that locked in that teenage head of yours is the key to a case that we are working on." "Whatever you say, Sheriff. Whatever you say."

CHAPTER SIX

*"She moved to push herself up as her
feet disappeared into the sedan."*

Hollywood Boulevard was quiet; it was just after two a.m., and Joanna Fines was half-drunk and walking home to her mother's apartment after a long night with some of her high school friends. She was standing at the corner of Hollywood and Laurel Canyon Boulevard, getting ready to cross the street. One of her friends drove by and stopped in front of her, rolled down the window and asked, "Jojo, are you sure you're okay? You really tied one on. You want me to drive you home?" "Tony…I live right there." She was pointing a wavy finger in the direction of her apartment building right across the street. "Okay…that was a hell of a sixteenth birthday party we threw for you. Are you sure you don't want to come with us back to my folks and crash? Your mother is probably gonna rip you a new one for getting hammered and being out all night. You can sleep it off, and I will have my mom call yours and tell her that we had a sleepover." Joanna giggled and said, "Shh…my mom isn't home. She won't get off work until six…I'm fine. Go home. I love you guys." "We love you, too!"

The light changed, and Joanna started across the street, her long slender Hispanic legs stretching the fabric of her tight fitting dress. She had her boobs on parade as she strolled the intersection to the other side. She made it to the corner, staggering, when a black sedan pulled up next to her. She turned to see the passenger window roll down and a male voice ask for directions. The voice was soft, and she yelled with slurred speech, "I'm sorry. I can't understand you...where do you want to go?" The voice remained low, and she moved closer to the passenger window, looking into the car. She got to the edge of the curb and asked, "Now try again. Where you are looking to go?" There were no other cars on the road, and the man spoke a little louder, but she couldn't make out all of what he was asking, though she picked up that he wanted her to come closer to the car. "No sir...my mommy told me never to get too close to a stranger's car. Why are you looking for an address in the middle of the night anyway?" She flung her arm forward and lost her balance, falling onto the passenger door of the car. Her upper half was in the passenger side window while her feet were on the street. She moved to push herself up as her feet disappeared into the sedan, and it sped off down the street.

Alan Holden got home a little past two a.m. He was tired, and he was scared. He unlocked the house and went in and sat down in the living room. He sat with his head in his hands for a few seconds and then went to get the luggage out of the car. He had just dropped Holly's bags at the guesthouse and was walking back into his own home when a black sedan pulled up to the front of the house. Holden looked over with bags in his hands and waved and walked on in. The sedan pulled to the back of the house near the garage, and there was some rustling around as Alan worked to open and unpack his bags. The doorbell rang, and he yelled out, "The door is open, Clive. Come in." Clive Montgomery came walking through the door. He was dressed in a pair of tan khaki shorts and a red Tommy Bahama shirt that was untucked. His dark black hair and chiseled features were only offset by his staggering green eyes. He was thin, standing five foot four, and Alan laughed when he saw him. "Green contacts tonight, Clive? Really? You have brown fuckin' eyes, man. What do you want? I'm wiped out." Clive walked in and helped Alan with the last of his luggage and asked, "Where's Holly?"

Alan sat down on his bed and with tears in his eyes told him what had happened. Clive sat down in a chair across from the bed listening as Alan talked. Clive looked at his watch; it was nearly three a.m. "So, are you afraid that Holly will tell them that you fucked her?" Alan got a pissed off look on his face and said, "You know, Clive, you can be an asshole. Yes, I'm afraid she's going to tell them. I don't want to go to jail, man!" Clive nodded, looking at Alan's handsome features lit up by the lamp in the room and the moonlight. "You're way too pretty for prison, dude!" "Oh fuck you, Clive...FUCK YOU! You are my second in command at the agency.

Why don't you try to give me some advice that will help me out?" Clive had a thoughtful look on his face. "I don't know what to say…Holly has been nabbed by the cops." "She's been nabbed by the FBI."

Clive's look turned somber. "What would the FBI want with you or Holly?" "This special agent was asking a lot of questions about the Hollywood murders." "What did you tell him?" Alan stood up and walked over to the wet bar in his bedroom and poured a drink and offered one to Clive, who accepted. "Nothing, man. Shit! Are you out of your mind? I pled the fifth, and Howard Cohen got me out of the interrogation room before the questions could go further." "So what now?" Clive asked, taking a sip of the drink. Alan swigged his drink down and poured another. He paced the bedroom looking out over the pool. "Fuck, Clive, I don't know. This has all been under the police's radar with the fires and all the other shit that has happened over the last year and half. If you hadn't taken that damn Strom girl, it would still all be under the radar."

Alan heard the mummer of a girl coming from the back of the house. He walked out the sliding glass doors to the garage where Clive had parked and looked in the back seat. He whipped around to see Clive right behind him. "Jesus Christ, Clive. This is, what, the third or fourth in two weeks. What the hell is going on?" Clive walked back to the rear door of the sedan and opened it. Joanna was laying on her back. She had a piece of duct tape over her mouth, her skirt had hiked up, and she wasn't wearing underwear. Her cleavage drew Alan's attention immediately. He told Clive to bring her into the house, so he threw the girl over his shoulder. When they got into the house, Clive threw Joanna onto Alan's bed, and she huddled up against the headboard. "Jesus, Clive. What is she? Fifteen? Sixteen?" "Just had her sixteenth birthday. I grabbed her at Hollywood and Laurel Canyon. Tell me that she is not one fine piece of ass … huh … tell me she's not."

Alan ran his hands down her legs. She jerked away from him, and he said, "Oh, a feisty little minx, I see." "How tall do you think, Clive?" He laughed, "Oh, shit, man, four foot six, four foot seven. She's a homunculus, Alan. She's perfect for you. You can feed your appetite, and when you're finished with her, I can feed mine." Holden paced the bedroom staring at Joanna lying on the bed. "We can't kill her right now, Clive. You will have to suppress your desires. I will have to suppress my own. There's too much attention on me right now. The cops don't know you exist. They have their eye on me. Take her to the sex room, and we will take pictures and have fun with her, BUT DO NOT INJURE HER!"

He nodded and threw her back over his shoulder. She was combative, and Alan said, "Hold on!" He grabbed a syringe out of the nightstand next to his bed and injected Joanna in the ass. She stopped flailing immediately. "There. Now I know she can't hurt you, and you can't hurt her. I swear, Clive, if she has so much as a bruise when I strip her to take photos I will beat you with a rubber hose." Clive nodded contritely and walked out of the bedroom. Alan watched as Clive walked through the moonlight and the light emitted down on his home from the Getty. Clive opened the second outbuilding and walked in with Joanna over his shoulder. He was in there for only a few minutes and came right back to Alan's bedroom. "Did you cuff her to the bed?" Clive nodded. "Okay, then get undressed for bed. I'm horny, and I might just as well take it out on your ass." Clive stripped off his clothes and slid down the middle of the bed until he was near the pillows. He pushed himself up onto his knees and put a pillow under his abdomen. "I have trained you well, Clive. Very, very well. Put some lube on your anus while I take a piss, then I will come back and fuck you. You deserve the punishment that I'm going to take out on your ass." Clive kept his head down as he reached over and groped for the nightstand drawer and did as instructed. Alan emerged from the bathroom nude and erect with a spiked cock ring covering half his penis. He shut off the lights and said, "This is going to hurt you, Clive, and I'm going to enjoy it." The only sound that could be heard was Alan grunting as Clive quietly wept in the darkness, his breath being taken from him with each powerful thrust of Alan's leather bound shaft.

Jim arrived home at two thirty with Jessica half-asleep in the passenger seat. He parked the car in the garage and walked around to the side door where Barbara was waiting for him. He had called ahead to let her know he was bringing a houseguest. The two got Jessica out of the car and into the house. Jim put her in one of his guest rooms where she undressed and went straight to bed, and he and Barbara walked into the living room and out onto the sundeck. "What makes you think this girl won't rob us blind or kill us in our sleep?" Barbara asked as Jim handed her a tumbler of scotch. "A hunch!" Barbara took a drink of the scotch and listened to the sea crashing on the shore below the deck. "Do you think she might be a lead in the Hollywood killings?" Jim lit a cigarette and offered it to Barbara, but she refused. He put it in his mouth, took a deep drag, and said, "I don't know…I just have a feeling this kid's life might be in jeopardy." "To be emancipated at her age, she must have had one hell of a bad home life." "She did, if her story is true, and based on my conversations with the kid, I have no reason to doubt her." They finished off the scotch and went to bed. Jim groped Barbara in the dark, and she turned on her side and said, "Have your way with me, big guy!"

John got home at two forty-five. All of the lights were on in the living room and the pool area. He walked out onto the deck, but there was no one there. He saw three robes on the floor, and he got a half smile on his face. He turned off the lights and walked back to the bedroom to find Sara asleep in bed. He undressed and slid into bed next to her. Her body was warm against his skin. He felt Sara's hand take a hold of his cock, and she rolled over on top of him and said, "Good morning, Agent Swenson…it's been a long week." He put his arms behind his head as Sara slowly slipped down under the covers. He closed his eyes with a smile on his face as she took him into her mouth.

It was half past four when Randy Strom pulled up and parked three houses down from where Hillary Sums and Terry Brady lived together. He got out of the car. He was in uniform and walked up to the front door and rang the bell. It took a few moments, but the lights came on in the main house, and then the porch light came on. Terry opened the door and upon seeing Randy began to scream, "Oh my God, no…please, God, no. Where's Hillary? Please, officer, tell me that Hillary's all right." His facial expression said it all, and Terry crumpled to the floor. Randy caught her as she fell. He helped her get to her feet and walked her back into the house. He held her in his arms as she wept, and he slowly closed the front door behind them.

CHAPTER SEVEN

*"Because if he doesn't, the Iron Eagle will
go get him, and it will be most unpleasant."*

The news of Hillary's death spread through the journalistic community like wildfire. By six a.m. the following morning, it was the running headline on every news source in the country. The facts were still sketchy on her death, but that didn't matter. As it is in all of American media, where they had holes, they filled them with lies. Freedom of the press now meant creative license as well, and they could always correct or retract if there was a glaring error. Pamela Bailey, the executive producer of *Los Angeles This Morning* and editor and chief of the newspaper, *Los Angeles Confidential,* was running hard and fast to get the news on the air and in print. Without facts, she printed the headline, '*Hollywood Killer Strikes Again, Takes One of Our Own!*' It was the lead story and had been leaked by an unidentified source, and the media was having a field day.

John was awakened by Sara just before seven with a bottle of Coke Zero and a smile. He sat up in bed and looked at her. She was radiant. "Well, it looks like someone had a great night's sleep!" John said with a laugh. Sara was drawing on John's peck with her finger, softly caressing his chest, speaking in a slow and sultry tone. "Is that a complaint, Mr. Swenson?" She was moving her finger across the scar where he had been shot. He shook his head, and she smiled. "You never told me how you got this wound." John sat up on the bed and whispered, "For the good of a nation." Sara knew what that meant. It meant leave it alone. It meant it was a wound he received in combat on some secret mission that he could never tell her about. John, the husband, was almost as much of an enigma as John the Special Agent and John the Iron Eagle. She pushed her head into his chest and nuzzled him deeply. He placed his hand on her head and smelled her hair. They held each other for only a few seconds before the home phone line was ringing. He reached over, holding Sara and his Coke in one hand and grabbed the phone.

"Swenson." "Have you seen the fucking news this morning?" "Jesus, Jim. Are you the paper boy?" "Someone leaked Sums' death. It's all over the news and in the papers." John sat up. "Someone? Someone? You and I both know who leaked the story." Sara was now out of bed and standing nude on the edge of the bedroom balcony getting ready to dive into the pool. Jim said, "Strom. That mother fucker. That son of a bitch leaked it to the press…and guess who they are blaming her killing on?" John didn't have to think about it; it just came out. "The Hollywood Killer!" "You got it, pal…the son of a bitch is trying to blame Sums' death on the Hollywood Killer. We need to do a press conference ASAP to correct this." John agreed. "I will have my office do a written press release immediately to kill the Hollywood Killer connection. We will do the news conference on the steps of my office building." Jim agreed, and they had their offices set up a joint press conference for nine a.m. with an immediate written press release debunking the whole notion that Sums' killing had anything to do with the Hollywood Killer. John got up and turned on the television, and the story was on every channel. He cursed under his breath, and Sara heard him.

"What's wrong sweetheart?" He walked nude to the deck where Sara was now sitting and told her the story from the night before. "So, you think someone leaked the story and misinformation to the media in order to draw attention away from the real killer?" "Yes…listen, honey, one of my law enforcement colleagues' daughter was recently murdered by the Hollywood Killer. The funeral is this morning at ten. Will you dress and accompany me to pay our respects?" "Of course, John, of course. How horrible. Do I know this person?" "Unlikely. His name is Randy Strom; he's a detective out of the Rampart division." Sara had a perplexed look on her face. John saw it and asked, "Do you know him?" She shook her head. "No, but I do know an Amy Strom. She's a clinical psychologist who does work at the hospital." John's head went down a bit. "The mother of the murdered girl is Amy Strom. The girl's name was Suzy." Tears began to run down Sara's face. "Are you okay?" Sara shook her head wildly. "Not by a long shot, John. I saw Amy yesterday before I left the hospital. She was preparing to do a group session for our domestic violence program, and she never said a word." "Perhaps she thought you had heard it from me?" "No. We made some very fast small talk and both commented on how little we see our husbands." John got up and went into the bathroom to shower. Sara followed. There was no conversation. They dressed and got in John's truck to head for his office. "I have to do a quick news conference, and then we will head for the church, okay?" Sara nodded. "Can you drop me back at the house after the service? I have some things I need to get done." John nodded as they pulled out of the parking garage and headed for PCH.

Jim pulled up in front of the federal building on Wilshire. The press was everywhere. Barbara was with him dressed in a dark colored suit. Jim pounded the steering wheel and let out, "Oh, fuck me, you sniveling bunch of scavengers." He was just reaching to open the car door when Barbara grabbed his arm. "I know you are emotional, Jimmy. Hold it back … press it back. Do this news conference, and then let's go to a much more somber and 'real' tragedy. A little girl is dead. Keep your focus on that and not on these animals." She leaned in and kissed his cheek. He opened the door and stepped out to the clicking of cameras and the shouting of questions from all directions. He saw John standing on a makeshift podium and approached dressed in full uniform. He shook John's hand and went to walk to the microphone when John pressed his hand into Jim's chest and stepped up instead. John was steady in his stance, deliberate in his delivery, direct and to the point.

"I will be making a quick statement and will be taking no questions, so everyone settle down and stop yelling. I am going to make this brief. The body of Ms. Hillary Sums was discovered in the upper level of an under construction high-rise building at approximately one forty-five a.m. this morning. Her immediate cause of death is under investigation by my office as well as the Los Angeles County Sheriff's Department with the cooperation of the Los Angeles Police Department and the coroner's office. There has been unsupported sensationalizing of this matter claiming that Ms. Sums was a victim of the Hollywood Killer. These claims are patently FALSE! I have ordered an immediate autopsy. Neither the FBI nor other law enforcement personnel in this matter believe that this is in any way connected to the Hollywood Killer. We will release more information on Ms. Sums' death when we feel it is not going to jeopardize the integrity of our investigation. Thank you."

John stepped away from the microphone and walked out to the parking lot and headed for Suzy Stroms' funeral with Jim right behind him.

The mood was somber at Our Sisters of the Holy Cross church on Euclid. There was standing room only, and Jim had gotten Barbara out of the car, and he had Jessica with them. The three walked quietly up the stairs of the great church. John and Sara were standing near the entrance when Jim approached. John looked over to see Jessica with him and asked, "Why is that kid with you?" "It's a long story. I will tell you later. Have you seen Randy?" He shook his head, and the two men looked on into the crowded church as a soft hymn played in the background.

John's imposing frame parted the standing crowd, and he made room for Sara and Jim as well as Barbara and Jessica three rows from the front of the church. A mahogany casket was set in front of the main alter. The lid was closed, and John and Jim knew why. There was a casket spray of roses in the middle with hundreds of other flowers filling the sanctuary. John saw Randy and Amy standing with some other attendees, quietly chatting near the front next to the casket. John stood up, and Randy made him right away. They locked eyes. Randy nodded a gentle nod to John who returned the gesture. The service went on until nearly eleven thirty. Nearly twenty people, young and old, talked about Suzy Strom. When the service ended, John and Jim along with Sara, Barbara, and Jessica followed the procession of people to the entrance of the church to pay their respects. Amy saw Sara and broke into tears. Sara wrapped her arms around her and whispered, "Why didn't you tell me?" Amy just shook her head. She was crying too hard to answer. Randy shook Jim's hand as John stood back. "We'll find him, Randy. I promise you we will find the bastard who did this!" He nodded shaking Jim's hand firmly. John waited until all of the mourners had paid their respects, and Randy and Amy were about to get into the limousine to take them to the cemetery. John walked up to Randy, and John could see the fear in his eyes. "I'm sorry for your loss, Randy. I know we have had our differences through the years, but your daughter's death is my top priority." Randy reached out his hand to shake John's, and John took it with a firmer than usual grip. He leaned in and whispered into his ear, "I know what you did!" Randy stood frozen. John continued, "We will find the animal or animals that did this, and he/they will be brought to justice. Don't step into this any further. You cannot move with immunity. You will do no one any good in prison or dead." John was squeezing Randy's hand so hard he had tears in his eyes, tears of pain. "After you have laid your daughter to rest, I want you to come to my office this afternoon at four. You and I need to have a chat. If you're not there, I will send someone to get you, believe me. You don't want me to have to do that." John released Randy's hand and walked over to Amy who was still holding Sara's hand. He gave his condolences, and then took Sara by the hand and walked her back to his truck. Jim had watched the exchange from a distance, and when John had put Sara into the truck he walked over and asked, "What the fuck was that all about?" "Be at my office at four. Randy will be there then as well." Jim laughed and said, "You really think that Randy Strom is going to come walking into the federal building and into the office of the FBI?" John nodded. "How the fuck can you be so sure?" "Because if he doesn't, the Iron Eagle will go get him, and it will be most unpleasant."

Jim said nothing. He just turned and walked back to his car. He was getting ready to get in when he called to John, "You have some errands to run before we meet?" John nodded. "You want some company?" John shook his head. Jim got into the car, and Barbara asked, "What the fuck is going on?" He was keenly aware that Jessica was sitting in the back seat of his car. "Just talking about an old Steve Miller band song." "Really? And what fuckin' song was that?" Jim smiled as he turned onto Euclid and answered, "Fly Like an Eagle." Barbara's face dropped, and Jessica saw it through Jim's rear view mirror. "Do you not like that song, Mrs. O'Brian?" Barbara turned in her seat as Jim headed back to their home. "You are way too young to have ever heard of that song." Jessica was sitting back in the seat looking out the window. "No. It's a great old song from like the twenties or something."

Jim started laughing, and Barbara turned around in her seat. "Did you hear that Barb? That song is from the 1920s. Jesus Christ, you're old!" She pressed her hand into Jim's leg, clenching his thigh with her fingernails. Jim let out a little yelp, which made Jessica laugh. "I don't know, Sheriff. I think you pissed off your wife. I bet you are going to have hell to pay for that." Jim glared into the rear view mirror, but all that did was draw a laugh from Barbara and Jessica. He kept his mouth shut as he drove Barbara home. When he got there he dropped her off, and had Jessica move to the front seat. Barbara asked, "What are you going to do with Jess?" "She's coming with me. I have some photographs I want her to look at." Jim drove off down PCH with Jessica looking out the window at the ocean, neither saying a word to one another.

CHAPTER EIGHT

"I don't know what type of axe you have to grind with him,
but I'm not going to help you sharpen it on my client's life."

Terry Brady was screaming into the darkness. She was gagged and handcuffed in a very small space. There was no light, and she tried to make as much noise as possible, but there was no noise outside of her own heavy breaths as she strained against the sides of her confinement.

It was noon when Alan and Clive parted ways. Alan warned him not to get near Joanna, and he nodded in agreement as Alan got into his Mercedes and headed for the office. Clive got into his car and was right behind him as they headed downtown.

Holly Bachman was sitting quietly in an office with a social worker who was typing away on a keyboard. She looked around for the attorney that had taken her from Alan the night before, but there was no sign of him. "Excuse me!" she said loudly. The woman looked up from her keyboard still typing away. "Where is the man who dragged me out of the federal building last night? I have a three o'clock with my hairdresser, and then I'm supposed to be on set to shoot a new episode of my show." The woman looked back down, her hands never stopping as they struck the keys on her computer. Holly was just about to start a fuss when a well dressed and bejeweled middle-aged black woman emerged from an office. The secretary stopped typing and looked at her and said, "Holly Bachman is here for you, Ms. Bandon." "I hear her. Ms. Bachman, would you come with me please?" "Not until you tell me who the hell you are and what's going on? I have to be on set. I have a contract, and if I violate that contract I can be sued as can my manager, Alan Holden." "I understand, Holly. You will be on set. Have no fear. I will take you." "Who the hell are YOU?" she yelled so loud that the typing stopped as did other background noise in the office. "My name is Anita Bandon, and I am, for all intents and purposes, your parent until such time as the court orders otherwise." "My guardian is Alan Holden. He's like a father to me. I don't understand why you people are doing this." Holly put her head in her hands, and Anita walked over and put her hand on her shoulder. "I don't understand all of this, Holly. We will get it worked out, and if you are supposed to be with Mr. Holden, you will be." "When...when will I know?" She was exasperated, and Anita softly asked her to rise and follow her. She did as asked, and Anita walked her down a long hall to a conference room. She invited her to have a seat, and when she stepped in, John was seated on the other side of the table.

"What is HE doing here?" she asked in anger. "This is Special Agent John Swenson with the FBI. He has asked to speak with you." "I'm not talking to him. He's the reason I'm here and not with Alan." John sat silent. "Mr. Cohen told me not to speak to this guy!" Anita pointed to a chair and asked her to sit. Holly did as she was asked, and Anita sat down next to her. "I'm your attorney right now. Agent Swenson is going to ask you some questions. I advise you to answer them." She shook her head, and John leaned forward in his chair and said, "Ms. Bachman, the sooner you answer my questions, the sooner you will be reunited with Mr. Holden. The longer you hold out, the longer you will be in the custody of Ms. Bandon. Now, do you want to answer a few simple questions, so you can move on with your life, or do you want to go to court and perhaps end up never seeing Mr. Holden again?" Holly started to cry, and Anita cautioned John not to make threats. "Agent Swenson, I agreed to allow this meeting because I thought it would help your investigation. If it is your intention to intimidate my client, I will urge her to stay silent, and I will request that the court reprimand you." John smiled and asked, "So ... what's it going to be, Ms. Bachman? Talk or court?" Holly shrugged her shoulders and asked, "What do you want?"

John pulled a gray folder out of his jacket and laid it on the table in front of him. "How long has Mr. Holden been your guardian?" "I don't know. Two, maybe three years." "Is there any legal paperwork that makes him that?" She shrugged. "Are you related to Mr. Holden?" She shook her head. "Then how did he become your guardian?" Holly was clearly pissed off. "I made him that, okay? I was on the streets; he picked me up, dusted me off, and gave me a life. He has fed me, clothed me, and helped me … in case you haven't noticed it, he has helped me launch a very successful modeling, acting, and singing career. I mean, you know who I am, right?" John nodded.

"Are you and Mr. Holden in a physical relationship?" Anita spoke up. "You will need to be more specific, Agent Swenson." "Are you having sex with or being forced to have sex with Mr. Holden for his help?" She turned her head and shrugged as she answered. "NO! For God's sake, he's my agent. He has not forced me to do anything. He takes care of me. He and Clive are the best people in the world. I would not be where I am today in my career without the two of them." John had his tablet out recording the conversation on video as well as audio. "Who is Clive?" She looked at Anita, who nodded that she needed to answer the question. "Clive is Alan's partner." "Business partner?" She nodded and said, "Amongst other things!" John sat up in his chair and asked, "Are you saying that Mr. Holden is in a physical relationship with this Clive person." Holly laughed and said, "Duh! Are you really that naïve? Alan is gay… well, not really all the way gay. He is mostly gay, but he likes girls, too, sometimes." "What is Clive's last name?" "Um…" Holly had her head in the air trying to search for it. "I really don't know him that well. I only know him as Clive." "And he is a business partner with Mr. Holden at his agency?" She nodded emphatically and asked, "Can I go now? Alan and I have a lot of deals in the works. If you want to know more about his love life, go see him and Clive. I'm sure they are at the office." John looked down at his tablet; it was a quarter to one. "Ms. Bandon will take you to your set and watch out for you today." John rose as he said it.

"Wait…you said if I answered your questions that I would be back with Alan, so you lied to me?" "No, Holly. I didn't lie to you, but I do need to speak with Mr. Holden and his lover, Clive. I need to know more about what they do." She got angry and started to yell at John. "What does Alan Holden's sex life have to do with me or our business relationship?" John was putting his tablet into a small bag when he asked, "Have you and Mr. Holden ever had sex?" Holly was rocked, and Anita saw the expression on her face before John did. "No…no, that's sick. I'm a kid. Why would he even think of having sex with me?" John looked up and said, "You're lying to me, Ms. Bachman. I will speak to Mr. Holden and this Clive fellow; however, I don't believe that you have not had sex with Mr. Holden." Holly got an indignant look on her face. "I live in his guest house; he runs every aspect of my career. Alan is a good, loving, and caring man. He loves Clive very much. He and I have not and do not have sex." Anita looked down at the table as John was walking for the door. Holly burst out in tears and said, "I want to go home. I want to go back to my life. I want Alan back. He has done nothing wrong. Why won't you believe me?" John was walking out the door as he answered, "You have been around Mr. Holden long enough that you have learned how to lie, Holly. Personally, if you have had consensual sex with Mr. Holden, I could care less … if you were of age. But you're not of age; you are sixteen, Ms. Bachman, and if you and Mr. Holden are having sex that is against the law. You are not in trouble for doing it; he is." "He didn't do anything wrong. I told you. He is my guardian, that's it. He's my manager and nothing more."

John walked out of the room with Anita behind him. John turned to her and said, "I'm sure she is sexually active, so a rape kit is not what is needed here. What I do need is to find out how many times she has had sex with Holden and then deal with him from that perspective." Anita had her hands on her hips as John spoke. When he was finished, she said, "Agent Swenson, I'm not a goddamn babysitter. This girl can be emancipated and should be. I see nothing wrong with anything that she has said. She has a career, and Mr. Holden helped her to get that. If you ask me, he helped a kid get off the street and gave her a life she might never have had. Mr. Holden is a role model that we should hold others up to. I'm setting a hearing for this afternoon to have Ms. Bachman returned to Mr. Holden. I don't know what type of axe you have to grind with him, but I'm not going to help you sharpen it on my client's life."

John looked at Anita and said, "Mr. Holden is a person of interest in the Hollywood murder investigation going on between my office and the sheriff's department. It is my job to profile killers, Ms. Bandon, and then catch them. You do what you like, but if Mr. Holden is indeed involved in this case, you could be sending Ms. Bachman into the hands of a killer. You think about that while you draft your brief for her to be released to him." She took her hands off her hips and got a serious look on her face. "Do you have any proof that Mr. Holden has done anything wrong?" He shook his head. "Do you have any proof that Mr. Holden is a threat to Ms. Bachman or others?" He shook his head again. "Agent Swenson, the law does not work on hunches or intuition; it works based on facts. You have no facts to support me doing anything but getting this kid back into the home that she knows and the person who she loves, and who appears to love her. I'm filing the motion for her release back to Mr. Holden this afternoon. If it turns out that you're right and Mr. Holden is a bad man, then it will be on my head. Right now, I have to do what I think is best for my client." And with that she walked back to Holly Bachman.

John called Jim after leaving Anita Bandon's office. "What?" "I just had a conversation with Holly Bachman." "Yea, and?" She claims that Holden is gay, and that he's involved with a man named Clive." Jim was sitting at his desk with Jessica sitting on the couch across from him. "Well, that's just diddly fuckin' great, John. So, the guy's a faggot. Did you get a last name for this Clive guy?" "No!" "Well, do you know where he works?" "Yea…he works for Holden." Jim laughed. "Then it won't be too hard to get the guy's last name and find out who he is." John was getting into his truck. He looked at the dash clock, and it was two thirty. "Listen, I have to run some more leads on Holden. Anita Bandon is Bachman's attorney, and she is releasing her back to Holden this afternoon. I've got Randy coming to my office at four. I need you to do some police work. See if you can get this Clive guy's last name and see if you can get any background on him." "Okay, and what are you going to do?"

Jim walked over to his stool with the cigarettes on it. He motioned to Jessica to see if she wanted a smoke, and she nodded and walked over to the window. "I'm going to check out Sums' home and talk to Terry Brady, her lover. I need to find out why Hillary Sums did something so reckless as fabricating a story about Randy's kid. I also need to make sure that Randy hasn't done anything else that he is going to regret." Jim let out a laugh and said, "I have a feeling that Randy is going to bring a world of hurt on him and his wife, not to mention anyone who disrespected his daughter's memory." John agreed as he heard the snap of Jim's lighter. "Where is the girl that you had with you this morning?" Jim looked at Jessica taking a hit off the cigarette he gave her. "She's with me; I think she might know more about this case than even she knows. I want to show her some mug shot books and see if she knows anyone." "Well, show her a picture of Holden and see if you can get one of this Clive guy. Maybe she has interacted with him or seen someone else interact with him, which could put a face to this killer." Jim said he would work on it after he hung up. John turned onto Lake Hollywood Drive in search of Sums' and Brady's residence, hoping he would find answers and not more questions.

Amy Strom was sitting at her desk in her home office when Randy walked in. He sat down in front of her desk and stared off into space. Amy was typing on her computer and pretending to ignore him. He looked on and could see that she was getting more and more aggravated with his presence. "We buried our daughter this morning, Randy. Our child is dead; she has been berated in the media, her memory insulted, and in the end it's all being made out to be Suzy's fault … and ours … that she was murdered." "Well, it's not, and you know that," he said in a somber voice. He stood up and paced. She stopped typing and started watching him. She waited for a few minutes and asked, "What have you done, Randy? Do you know who killed Suzy?" He shook his head. Amy continued, "I know you far too well, mister. You are feeling guilty. It is written all over your face. What's going on?"

He sat down again but didn't make eye contact. "I grabbed the reporter who wrote that horrible story about Suzy." Amy stopped everything and put her hands on her desk. "You're talking about Hillary Sums, who was found murdered this morning?" He nodded. "You killed her?" He nodded more slowly. "'Pressed' to death was what you said killed her. Is that right?" "Yea." "Do you feel better? Do you know who killed our daughter?" He stood up again and started pacing. "I'm not feeling any remorse over killing her, if that's what you mean, and no, I have no idea who killed Suzy or the other children." "You should have spoken to me before you made such a reckless move, Randy. You put your life, our life, in jeopardy over a news reporter? That's really irrational behavior. If you had found the killer and killed him I could understand and support that, but to kill a news reporter? I knew something was up when the FBI and the sheriff's department made a very, very quick press release disavowing the link between the Hollywood Killer and the killer of Ms. Sums. So, what now Randy? Who are you going to kill now? Hillary Sums was one of a hundred reporters who have reported junk about our child. Are you going to kill them all, or are you going to find the man who killed our child?"

Randy stopped in front of one of two picture windows in Amy's office and said, "I took Ms. Sums' lover…" Amy didn't move. "Is she dead?" He shook his head. "You can't kill her, Randy. You just can't do that. You are crossing a line from which there is no return. Do you want to end up like the Iron Eagle? Hunted by every law enforcement agency in the land?" Randy didn't turn around as he responded, "I'm not anything like the Iron Eagle. I don't go around killing other killers for the thrill of the hunt. I want to avenge Suzy's death. I thought that killing Sums would do that, but I know that it was wrong, and it didn't make me feel any better. I'm glad to get a piece of trash like her out of the news business, but it won't bring Suzy back." Amy got up and walked across the room to Randy standing in front of the window. She put her arms around him from behind and asked, "Does Ms. Sums' lover know who you are?" He nodded. "I went to her home after I killed Sums and broke the news to her, then I abducted her, and now I don't know what to do." Amy put her head on his back while she embraced him. "I really wish you would have spoken to me first on this. You have made a real mess." "It gets worse!" Amy released her grip on Randy and stepped back, "How much worse?" "John Swenson with the FBI has taken over the killing of Sums. He also wants me in his office at…" He looked at his watch; it was three thirty. "Four p.m. today for a meeting." "Why?" "I think he suspects that I had something to do with Sums' death." Amy paced for a few seconds and said, "Don't go. Make an excuse!" He shook his head. "If I don't show up, he will just hunt me down. I have to face him and let the chips fall where they may."

Amy walked around her desk, opened the top desk drawer, and pulled out a .357 Magnum she kept for protection. It had been an anniversary gift from Randy for their 20th last fall. She grabbed her handbag and slipped the gun into it and asked, "Where is Ms. Sums' lover?" "I have her hidden." "Take me to her." Randy turned around, and she was standing with her bag over her shoulder. "I don't want you involved." "Too late, Randy. It's too late for that. Take me to where you have her." He walked out of her office, and she followed him out to his car.

"You will need to meet with Agent Swenson at four. If you don't, it will bring the wrath of hell upon you and me. Take me to…," she had a thoughtful look on her face, "what's Ms. Sums' lover's name?" "Brady…Terry Brady." She frowned as they pulled out of the driveway of their home. "Great. That's just great. You had to grab not only the lover of a woman you killed, but a woman who is a patient in one of my domestic battery groups." He drove on from their home in Woodland Hills to a self storage center at the corner of Topanga Canyon Boulevard and Plummer Street. "Give me the passcode card for the storage container." Randy pulled out his wallet and took out a blue card with writing on it. He had a half consumed bottle of water in his cup holder, and she asked for it. He handed her the bottle of water and the card. "I will make my way back to the house. You get down to Swenson's office. I will take care of things with Terry." "What are you going to do?" "She's my patient. I will figure out something that will keep us both out of trouble. Call me when you're done with Swenson." She closed the passenger side door and ran across the street to the storage yard. Randy watched as she walked up to the key pad on the outside of the building and put in the code to disarm the security on their unit. The storage building was eight stories, and their unit was at the very top. He watched Amy until she disappeared through the sliding doors of the building then took off for downtown and John Swenson's office.

Jim had picked up some sandwiches for himself and Jessica, and they were eating lunch in his office as he waited for the information he had found out about Clive Montgomery. He asked Jessica if the name meant anything to her, but she just shrugged, shaking her head. It was three fifteen, and he knew he needed to be at John's office at four. "Why are you being so kind to me, Sheriff?" Jess asked with a mouth full of food. "I'm not. I think that you might be the key to helping us put together a case, and I don't want you getting your ass fucked up on the streets or killed before I can put my hunch to the test." She laughed, taking a drink of the diet drink he had gotten her. "I get fucked up the ass every day, sometimes all day, literally. I like it, Sheriff. It's one of my big money moves for my johns. They will pay big bucks for it. I waive my little ass in their faces then tell them they can stick their cocks up it!"

Jim was in the middle of a bite of sandwich when she said it, and for just a fraction of an instant, he heard Barbara in his head, talking about what she loved in sex. "That's not the same thing, kid. Getting fucked up the ass because you're a prostitute is your deal, and I'm sure you are paid well for it. The fucking I'm talking about is metaphorical." Jess laughed again, and said, "I may not have graduated from high school, but I do understand metaphor from literal. You think that this Hollywood Killer guy is going to take me, don't you?" Jim nodded with a mouth full of meatball sandwich. He had red sauce on his cheeks, and Jessica laughed and leaned over with a napkin. "You look like a little kid when you eat like that!"

He took the napkin from her hand and cleaned his face. He was about to respond when there was a knock on his office door, and his secretary brought in a gray case file. "Are these the photos I wanted on the two men?" She nodded and walked out. "Okay, Jessica, it's time for you to earn your money. He put his sandwich down and opened the folder. There were two really good head shots of Holden and Montgomery from the California Department of Motor Vehicles. He got up and walked over to his desk and took out a large black book and with his back to Jessica put the two head shots in with about a hundred others. He closed the book and walked back over to the coffee table they were eating lunch on and said, "I want you to look through this book and point to any men that you recognize. She was cleaning her hands with a wet wipe when she asked, "Are there any photographs of guys who were picked up for solicitation?" Jim got a confused look on his face. "I only ask because if there are, I'm going to know a lot of the faces in your book." She laughed when she said it.

"I hadn't thought of that. Fuck me." He thought for a few seconds. It was getting close to time for him to leave to go to John's office. He cleaned up the lunch and put the book under his arm and said, "You're coming with me." "Where to now, Sheriff?" "I have a meeting with the FBI, and I don't want to let you out of my sight. I'm going to give you this book, and I want you to look through it. Forget about the johns. I want you to point out any men you might have seen or talked to that were not clients of yours." They were walking out of the building as Jim handed her the book. "Well, that should narrow it a bit. What if they were both?" Jim was pulling a cigarette out of his top left pocket after starting his car. "What do you mean?" he asked, lighting the smoke and handing her one without even asking. "I mean, what if I have done business and pleasure with them?" "Mark those with this red marker. For the love of God, make sure you know what you did with them outside of the sack." There was a laugh as they headed for John's office.

CHAPTER NINE

"How did you find me?" "Quite by accident,
I can assure you, quite by accident."

Alan Holden was sitting at his desk when Howard Cohen arrived. He jumped up and opened the door for him. It was just a little after four p.m. "Please tell me that Holly is being released back to me!" Howard sat down in one of the office chairs and said, "The hearing was a little over an hour ago. The judge didn't want to rule from the bench but promised we would have an answer by five p.m." "What do you think will happen?" Howard sighed and said, "I think she will be released back to you with restrictions." "What kind of restrictions?" "You will need to file a formal petition for guardianship or allow the court to make her an emancipated minor." Alan had a confused look on his face. "Would that mean that she would be seen as an adult in the eyes of the law?" Howard nodded, and Alan smiled. Howard looked at him sternly and said, "You and I need to talk about what's going on between you and Special Agent Swenson." "I have no idea, Howard. He has some bizarre fascination with me. He is pressing me over the Hollywood killings." "And why do you think he is doing that?" Alan sat down behind his desk and said, "I can tell you exactly why he's pressing me. My business card ended up in the possession of one of the victims. Ever since then he has been pressing me." "How did your card end up in the hands of a victim?" Alan opened a bottle of water on his desk and offered one to Howard who refused. "I ran into the kid and her mother, like…months ago at the beach. I vaguely remembered giving her mother a card. Because the girl was cute, I thought she would make a great model. Mom said no, but I gave her my card anyway, and I gave one to the kid. That's how I came to be a 'person of interest.'"

Howard took out a legal pad and started writing. "What are you doing?" Alan asked with a mouth full of water. "Taking notes." "Why?" "Because the fact that your business card ended up in the possession of a victim of a serial killer is relevant and makes you a suspect." Alan slammed the bottle down on his desk as he responded, and Clive walked in. "I'm not a damn person of interest, Howard. Jesus, man. If this is going to make me a suspect in this kid's death, you might just as well round me up for anything that goes wrong with any teenager between twelve and eighteen because that's my market in the modeling business. I hand out my card to dozens of people every day." Howard was making notes but not looking at Alan. Clive greeted Howard, whose head was in his legal pad, and Howard acknowledged him with a quick, "Oh, hello, Clive. How are you today?" Clive looked on at Alan and could see he was seething with anger. "What's going on, Alan?" "Howard stopped in to tell me that Holly should be back with us shortly and to ask me questions about why Agent John Swenson of the FBI has an interest in me." Clive smiled and said, "Well, maybe Agent Swenson is gay, and he thinks you're a stud, so he's using this as an excuse to get close to you." There was sarcasm and jealousy in his words. Howard laughed, and Clive asked what was so funny. Howard stopped writing for a few seconds and said, "Not to pop any ego balloons here, but I know Special Agent Swenson and his wife personally. Agent Swenson is not gay. If you are on his radar, you're on it because he suspects something and that should give you cause for concern."

Alan stood up and said, "Well, shit, Howard. If you know Agent Swenson so damn well, why don't you go meet with him, and let him know I run a legitimate business, and that I only look out for the well being of my clients." Howard shook his head as he was back to writing again. "It's not that easy, Alan. I will need your itinerary for the past month." "What the hell for?" "You let me worry about that. Just get it for me, so I can go over it and compare your whereabouts with the murders in the past month. If I can provide Agent Swenson with an iron clad alibi for your whereabouts, he might go away." Alan got excited and ordered his secretary to email Howard all the information he requested. Howard stood up and said, "Don't celebrate any victory yet. Agent Swenson is a savvy and dedicated public servant. You're on his radar, and until I can prove without a doubt you don't belong there, you better cross every T and dot every I." Howard thanked the men for their time and walked out of the office.

Clive sat down and said, "You're in the clear. You raped the girls, but I did the killing, so you're covered. There is no way to connect you to anything." Alan took a drink of his water and said, "Stay away from Joanna, Clive, until we know we are in the clear. If Agent Swenson is as good at his job as Howard just said, he is watching us like a hawk. We should both assume for the time being that we are being followed everywhere." Clive nodded in agreement. When Alan's phone rang there were a few moments of silence, and he let out a howl of joy. "That's wonderful news, Ms. Bandon. I will be down to pick up Ms. Bachman right away." He hung up the phone and looked at Clive and said, "The judge ruled in my favor. Holly is coming back home tonight. I need to get over to pick her up before the attorney closes her office." Clive's facial expressions said it all, and Alan walked over to him, grabbed his face, and gave him a long, deep, passionate kiss. "Holly is my client. You are my love!"

Clive nodded weakly as Alan left the room and when the door shut he murmured to himself, "She can take you from me though. I know it. It's happened before. You always come back to me, but you have been lead astray before." He drummed his fingers on Alan's desk and spoke to himself in the form of a question, "Why can't I just cut out the middle man with Joanna? I can have some fun, kill her, and then store her body at the house. Alan won't know and even when he finds out, he always forgives me. I so desire to inflict pain." Clive grabbed a letter opener off of Alan's desk and stabbed it into his right arm. He smiled as the steel blade stuck out of his flesh, and a small stream of blood ran down his forearm. "That will do for the moment!" He pulled out the letter opener, cleaned off the blood, and put it back. He covered his arm as he left Alan's office heading for his own.

Amy Strom made her way up to the eighth floor of the storage facility then unlocked the padlock and opened the unit. She could hear the murmured screams of Terry Brady coming from a blanket that she was wrapped in. Amy drank the rest of the water then looked around the container for Randy's 'fix it kit.' She found it and pulled out a roll of duct tape. There was a large leather sofa near where Terry was. Amy took out the .357 and placed the plastic bottle over the barrel of the gun and duct taped it onto the barrel. She moved several throw pillows that were stacked near the couch then slowly removed Terry's bindings. When Terry's head was exposed, she was dripping with sweat and teary eyed. She looked up at Amy who pulled the duct tape off her mouth. She began to speak loudly, and Amy cautioned her to keep her voice down. Terry's face grew grim when she asked Amy, "Are you friend or foe, Amy?" Amy smiled a reassuring smile and said, "Friend, Terry, always friend. I just learned that you had been abducted, and I wanted to come and talk to you about it." Terry had a strangely calm expression on her face, and she said in a soft voice, "How did you find me?" "Quite by accident, I can assure you, quite by accident."

Jim and Jessica arrived at John's office at the same time Randy did. They all went through security together. Jessica was engrossed in the mug shot book that Jim had given her, and she was making marks on nearly every page as she moved to the elevator with the two men. "Who's this?" Randy asked. "An intern. She is thinking about going into police work when she gets out of college, and my department is sponsoring an informal introduction to law enforcement." Randy laughed and said, "Now that is the biggest bunch of bull shit I have ever heard come out of the mouth of Jim O'Brian. You fucking hate kids, and you have no patience for pretense. You would have pawned this off on one of your people." He looked Jessica up and down and then leaned into Jim and whispered, "You're fucking that, aren't you?"

The look on Jessica's face never changed as she responded to Randy's question. "Yep, he's fucking me. I'm his personal sex toy, and his wife's, too. Now, can you talk about something else? I'm trying to concentrate." Jim let out a deep belly laugh as the elevator doors opened, and the three stepped off at John's floor to be greeted by two field agents. Jim looked at the two men but didn't recognize them. "Well, John has some new blood I see. This is unusual. John meets me on his own." There was no response as they all followed the men to a secure conference room where John was waiting. John stood up and waved the two agents off, and all of them entered the room." John looked at Jessica and then asked Jim, "Did you get the information on the other guy?" Jim nodded. "Has she told you anything yet?" He shook his head. Jessica never took her eyes off the book as she was making a note on one of the photographs. "Didn't anyone ever tell you it is rude to speak of a person in third person when he or she is present?" Jim smiled as did John, and he apologized. He called one of the agents back and asked him to take Jessica to a holding room while the three men talked. Jessica walked off out of the room and called out to Jim. "Do I get to spend the night with you and Barbara again, Sheriff?" Both John and Randy shot him a look as he responded, "It depends on what you can tell me from that book." She was still within earshot when he heard her say, "I'm going to bet that I will be staying with you and your wife again tonight." Randy looked at both men whose faces remained stoic. "Please sit, Randy," John asked as Jim closed the door.

Alan Holden made his way to Anita Bandon's office, got through security and into the waiting area where he saw Holly. She jumped up, ran across the room, and threw herself into his arms. "Are you okay, Holly?" "I am now. I just heard that I get to go home with you." Alan nodded as Anita entered the room. She invited the two into her office and went over the conditions. When she had finished, Alan looked at his watch; it was half past five. He thanked Anita for her assistance and left with Holly and a stack of documents that he had to read and fill out. Anita warned that his custody of Holly was only temporary. The judge had agreed to allow it for two weeks, and if the forms weren't back and the requirements met, then Holly would be remanded back to the state, though Anita said that she was expecting to receive Holly's emancipation order from the judge at any moment, which would make all of the paperwork moot.

Alan asked what the emancipation would mean, and Anita explained that an order of emancipation would in essence make Holly an adult in the eyes of the court and the law. She could do everything that an adult could do with the exception of smoke until she reached the age of eighteen or drink alcohol until she is twenty one. Outside of that, she must support herself, which she was doing with her acting and modeling, and not commit any crimes. As Holly and Alan were getting ready to leave the office, word came down that Holly had been emancipated by the court and that there was no reason for the paperwork. Alan handed the documents back to Anita and asked if there was anything else he needed to do. Anita looked at him and said, "For all intents and purposes, Holly Bachman is now an adult; however, you took it upon yourself to take Holly under your wing, Mr. Holden, and made her the celebrity she is today. Her money belongs to her, and you must set up bank accounts and all other financial matters in her name. You should also make sure that she has a good accountant and lawyer. She might look like an adult and be treated by the state as an adult, but believe me, she's not one yet." He promised to look after her as he had been doing, and as they left the building Holly looked at Alan and said, "Now we can have sex, and you can't get in trouble, right?" He nodded, and she clapped her hands together like a little kid.

Clive was driving back to Alan's house, and he voiced only one desire. "I want to make that little cunt suffer." He was hoping to beat Alan back to the house, so he could grab Joanna and take her somewhere where he could do what he liked with her while leaving Alan out of the pleasure of her company and her killing altogether.

Terry Brady sat silently on the leather couch in the climate controlled storage container rented by Randy and Amy Strom. Amy sat next to her with her hand on her knee trying to both console and convince. "I know how this looks, Terry, but I assure you that Randy was trying to protect you. He had been at the crime scene after Hillary had been killed. He told me that he didn't trust anyone in this situation, and he feared for your safety." Terry sat calmly listening to Amy as she tried to explain her husband's bizarre actions. Amy finally quieted down, and Terry asked, "If your husband is so worried about my safety, why would he bring me to a storage container handcuffed with duct tape over my mouth? I'm trying to understand, Amy. I really am. I know that Hillary made some really poor decisions in the way she reported your daughter's death. Believe me when I tell you that our last words before she was so brutally murdered were not pleasant ones. I'm not kidding, and I will have to live with that for the rest of my life. When your husband showed up at my front door last night, I knew that Hillary was dead. He hadn't said a single word, but I knew. Hillary…WAY OVERSTEPPED the boundaries of decency in regards to your daughter. I had no idea Randy was your husband. You don't talk about your personal life in sessions."

Amy smiled and said, "You don't know how hard it has been to keep this inside. No one I worked with knew that Suzy was my daughter. Randy insisted that we keep a really, really low profile all of the years that we have been married. Outside of administration at her schools and her medical care, I can count on one hand the people that knew that Suzy was the daughter of a police officer. When Randy made detective and started working homicide, things got worse. He not only had to protect his family, but he was seeing the brutality of man on man. It became overwhelming. He is a protector at heart, and I know that when he got to you to tell you the news there was a part of the protector in him that turned on and he did, while not rational, what he thought he needed to do to protect you." Terry looked on at Amy's tear-stained face, and her expression of anger turned to one of understanding.

"We buried our baby this morning, Terry." Her stare now turned to one of compassion, and Terry reached to hug her in a moment of comfort. "I still have to deal with that for Hillary, and I don't know how I'm going to handle it." The two embraced, and after a few moments of tears Terry asked, "Do you think I'm in danger?" Amy looked her in the eye and said, "I don't think so. I think that Randy overreacted. I think you are safe. I'm sure you want to get out of here and go home." Terry nodded. Amy paused and asked, "How are you going to deal with this with the press and your job?" Terry smiled and said, "Oh, that's no problem at all. I don't think that anyone even knows that I'm missing at this point. Those who know me will not be surprised that I have been out of contact for nearly twenty four hours. Believe it or not, there is respect even in the media room."

Amy smiled a weak smile and asked, "Will you forgive Randy for what happened, or is this going to make the major news networks and papers?" Terry smiled at Amy and said, "I'm flattered that Randy would think so much of me as to go to such great lengths to protect me. Granted, a hotel or motel room under an alias would have been better, but I understand he was and still is under great duress. Now that I know you know about this, I say let's just let this go." Amy sighed a sigh of relief and said, "Let's get you home. You have so much to do, and you have your own grief to deal with." They walked out of the storage container, and Amy shut it and locked it, then the two walked out of the unit. Amy walked out of the building and called for a taxi. What she did not realize was that all of her movements had been being caught on closed circuit security cameras. Every move she made from the moment she entered the container to her and Terry Brady getting into the cab at the entrance. From the moment Amy Strom typed in her security code to enter the container to typing it in again to lock it, she had left a perfectly documented trail of her actions and the whereabouts of Terry Brady.

CHAPTER TEN

*Clive pulled the door open and entered,
closing it quickly behind him, shutting out
Joanna's screams at his sudden presence*

Alan Holden arrived home at just before six p.m. with Holly by his side. He took her down to the guest house and told her to shower, and they would go out for dinner. He walked back to the main house, and as he did, Clive pulled up in front. He got out of the car, and Alan asked what he was doing at the house so early. "You might not want to play with the new toy I got you last night, but it needs food and water to stay alive." Alan nodded as Clive took a steel pie plate and put some wet dog food on it and filled a steel bowl with water and started for the front door. Alan looked at Clive and said, "Listen, we have had a long day. I know that you are stressed. Why don't you feed it, and then come and join me and Holly for dinner, okay?" Clive was a little evasive but finally agreed. He asked if he could strip the girl and collar and chain her to the bed frame and take off the wrist restraints. "Yes…but remember that Holly is down at the guest house, so keep the door shut, so her cries don't get out. You can strip her and beat her down into submission, so she eats, then get over here so we can have dinner."

Clive said defiantly, "You know that it takes more than five minutes to beat the will out of even the youngest of the toys." Alan huffed. "Strip her, whip her, and let her know this is all the food she gets until she learns to behave. Leave the food and water near the end of the chain, so she has to struggle to get it..." Alan threw his hands down to his sides and said, "I don't have to explain this to you. You know what to do. Just don't leave permanent marks. I want to fuck a clean, fresh skinned girl not a beaten piece of meat." Clive turned with a dejected look on his face, and Alan called out to him, "Hey? I'll make you a deal. You strip, collar, and feed her, and when we get home and Holly goes off to bed, you and me will go out and play with her. How about that?" A sadistic smile grew across Clive's face. "So, don't hurt her, Clive. Just scare her. I will have my way with her, then I'll give her to you tonight to do with as you please." Now the smile was all the way across Clive's face. He walked out the front door headed for the outbuilding knowing that Alan had never lied to him when it came to playing with the toys. He would have a few minutes of fun now and would wait for the ecstasy later. Clive pulled the outbuilding door open and entered, closing it quickly behind him, shutting out Joanna's screams at his sudden presence.

John and Jim, for the most part, had been making small talk with Randy. John was trying to show sensitivity to Strom, knowing he had buried his daughter only a few short hours earlier. After a few minutes of back and forth, Randy asked, "We are not old friends, gentlemen. Why am I here?" John looked at Jim who took out a cigarette from his top pocket and stuck it in his mouth. John leaned forward onto the conference room table and said, "I know for a fact that you killed Hillary Sums!" Jim didn't make a move. Randy sat staring at John in stunned silence for a fraction of a second and then said in defiant anger, "How dare you make such a bold and absolute statement like that. I have been a police officer for nearly three decades, and I'll be goddamned if I'm going to sit in the office of the fucking FBI and be accused of murder." John sat back in his chair, and Jim just sat chewing on his cigarette with no reaction.

"Randy, have you spent much time on Ernst construction sites?" He had a blank look on his face when John asked the question. "Ernst Construction is one of the world's leading high rise construction companies. Michael Ernst, the owner of the company, is a real keen business owner. All of his construction sites are monitored by remote security cameras literally set all over the location. The company started doing this after being sued by several different employees and subcontractors for miscellaneous and frivolous things. Ernst also uses the cameras to monitor equipment and materials. Take copper pipe and wiring, for instance. People steal that off sites all the time and make a huge profit selling it in the recycling market." Randy was clearly getting frustrated as John spoke and finally asked, "What does any of this have to do with me?" John pulled out his tablet, pressed a button, and turned it in Randy's direction. There, on the screen, was Hillary Sums with Randy standing over her, stacking concrete blocks on her chest. He didn't say a word. John took the tablet back and looked at the screen and said, "Very sloppy, Randy, very sloppy. You killed the woman on camera. Oh…and I have been able to get some great close-ups." Randy slumped down in the chair and put his hands out on the table.

"But how could you have known? And how did you get access to the security tapes so quickly?" John didn't miss a beat. "I saw the cameras and hacked their system remotely while on scene. Jim didn't even know I had done it. I've been a cop for a few decades, too, Randy, and I'm also a well trained countersurveillance operative." Randy's eyes filled with tears. "She lied about my child; she wasn't even apologetic about it. She just wanted to sell newspapers and TV spots." John looked on as Jim stood up and walked out of the room. "So, you got me. I did it. I will make a full confession." John sat back and asked, "Why go after a reporter when it's the killer you want brought to justice?" Randy gave a biting retort. "Because we either never catch these animals or when we do we coddle them. They get carried by the hand through the justice system, and in the end, end up with book deals and movies being made about their exploits. And what does my daughter get out of it? Nothing. She's still dead. So, I executed justice in the only way I could. I took it out on the misinformation of the media, more accurately the lies of Hillary Sums."

Amy had the driver take her home, so she could get her car and drive Terry home. When they pulled into Terry's driveway, Amy asked if she could use her phone as her cell phone battery had died. Terry gladly accommodated her, and the two women walked into the house. Terry handed Amy a phone while she walked into the living room to pick up some items she had dropped the night before. Amy looked around the room and saw throw pillows on the couch. She picked one up and pulled the gun from her purse. Terry's back was to Amy when she said, "I'm so sorry about all of this, but it is for the best." Terry turned to face her saying, "What's for the best?" Those were the last words that Terry Brady uttered as Amy Strom pushed the pillow into her face and fired the gun. Terry hit the floor like a ton of bricks; there was no sound as the bullet exited the gun and entered Terry's brain, uniting her with Hillary once more.

Jessica was sitting in one of the other interrogation rooms still looking at the mug shot book when Jim walked in. She looked up as her hand was marking yet another photograph and saw a look of dissatisfaction and something else she couldn't put her finger on. "You don't look very happy, Sheriff." He sat down across from her and asked if she had found anything. She nodded and told him mostly johns that she had done over the years. She handed the book to Jim, and he flipped through the pages until he came to the page where he had put in photographs of Holden and Montgomery. Next to Alan's name she wrote, 'Great photographer. Did several porn shoots and nudes with him last year.' Next to Clive's name were the words, 'Gay hooker.' Jim put the book down with the pages open and asked, "Tell me about these two men." Jessica looked on and said, "Not much to tell. The first guy is Alan Holden. He's a photographer I met about a year ago. He promised to make me a star, and he did … in a way." Jim asked her how. She laughed and told him he made her a porn star. Jim looked at her with a dead stare and said, "You can't be a fuckin' porn star; you have to be eighteen." She started laughing when Jim said it. "I'm a porn star in a very, very special industry." Jim said it before she could get the words out. "The child porn industry!" She nodded and told him it paid good.

"How many photo shoots and films did you do with Mr. Holden?" Jessica got a thoughtful look on her face. "Oh…ten films, and I don't know, hundreds of photographs." "Do you know where I can find your films and pictures?" "You're not a pedophile are you, Sheriff?" He shook his head. "Of course not, but if you have a URL or HTTP site, I can cross check it and maybe save other children from this sicko." There was a pad of paper on the table with a cup full of pens, and she wrote down three URLs. "Now, if I find out you wanted this just to beat off to naked pictures of me, I'm going to be pissed. If you want me, you can have me." He shook his head as he took the paper from her and said, "I don't want to fuck you, kid. I'm trying to help you. Who is the other guy?" "He used to work the strip with a lot of other guys, at least that's what he told me when I was working with him and Alan on some shoots. He and Alan are an item, and Alan got him off the streets and cleaned him up. From what I recall, they are a couple." Jim looked down at the photographs and the notes for a few more seconds then stood up with the book and the piece of paper in hand and said, "Don't fuckin' move." He darted out of the room.

John and Randy were in a quiet stare down when Jim came bolting into the room. "I need you now, John!" He got up and told Randy to stay put. He followed Jim into the hallway and asked what was up. Jim handed John the book and said, "I had Jessica look at these shots, and it turns out that Alan Holden is not just a photographer, but he is also a kiddy porn producer and distributor." John looked at the photos and Jessica's writing next to them. "Where is she?" Jim pointed down the hall, and John walked briskly to the integration room. He talked to Jessica, and she told him the whole story. When she was finished, John looked at Jim and said, "I want you to take Randy into custody but don't charge him. Keep it low key and wait for my call."

John took off out of the building, and Jim had a pretty good idea where he was going. He walked back to the interrogation room and cuffed Strom. "Where's Swenson?" "He had to run out on another case. He asked me to take you into custody." Randy didn't resist as Jim walked him out of the building with Jessica behind him.

CHAPTER ELEVEN

"If there is a development, where are we going?"
Jim said, "To the fuckin' development."

The Eagle pulled up and parked out away from Holden's home. He pulled on his mask and grabbed a duffle bag of equipment. He marked the time; it was eight p.m. The street was dark; the only light came from the Getty Center. He moved through the darkness with ease. He got to the outbuilding he had checked before, but it was just as it had been. He moved over to the second outbuilding and looked at the door; it had a magnetic lock. The Eagle pulled out a remote sensor and picked up the code right away. He heard the lock click and pulled the door open slowly.

Alan, Clive, and Holly had finished their meals and were heading back to the house. Holly was talking nonstop about being an adult, and how she could finally move on with her life thanks to Alan and Clive. When they got back to the house, Holly was frisky with Alan, and he could see that Clive didn't like it. Alan kissed Holly and said to the two of them, "The only way I think that we can all be happy is to have a threesome." Clive nodded, and Holly just looked on and asked, "What's a threesome?" Alan laughed and explained to her that it was an adult way of expressing love for more than one partner at the same time. "Oh, that's gross, Alan," she said, walking up to the house. "It's not gross, Holly. You just haven't tried it. Trust me, you will enjoy it." She asked, "Can I try it in the morning? I'm beat. It's been a pretty trying past few days, and I've only been an adult for a few hours." Alan smiled and kissed her on the forehead and told her that was fine. He told Clive to stay in the living room while he took Holly down to the guest house and got her to bed.

Clive paced impatiently waiting for the reward for his good behavior. Alan came back into the room and could see it on Clive's face and in his eyes. "You want what I promised?" He nodded his head slowly with a sinister smile." "Let's go. You earned this." The two men took off up the walk to the outbuilding to have their way with Joanna. When they got to the entrance door Alan said, "I get to have fun with her first. You will do the filming, so we can upload the images to our site, and then you can take her to the other building and do what you like to her." Clive nodded as Alan pressed a remote on his key ring, and the lock clicked open. Alan opened the door and turned on the lights only to find that Joanna was not in the room. Alan turned to scream at Clive only to find him seizing on the ground. He ran toward him when he saw the silhouette of a man in the doorway. The shadow that was cast from the Getty Center and streetlights outside was long, and Alan looked up to see a huge man with nothing but a black face. He didn't get a word out before he was hit with a taser and was on the ground next to his lover. He felt a sharp pain in his groin before he passed out. The Eagle carried the unconscious men to his truck and put them in the back. He checked the main house and the guest house. The Eagle could see Holly Bachman sleeping in her bed. He made no move for her. He simply walked back and drove off down to PCH headed for his lair.

Jim had no sooner pulled into police parking at the sheriff's station when his cell phone rang. "WHAT?" Randy and Jessica looked on as he sat both motionless and silent. He hung up the phone and turned the car around and pulled back out onto the street. Randy, who was sitting in the back seat handcuffed, asked, "Where are we going?" Jim didn't look at him through the rearview mirror as he replied. "I have been notified that there has been a development in the death of your daughter." Randy sat silent in the back seat, but Jessica asked, "If there is a development, where are we going?" Jim said, "To the fuckin' development."

Amy Strom walked into her own home after leaving Terry Brady's body on her living room floor with a bullet in her head. She walked directly into the laundry room, removed her clothes, and threw them into the washing machine then headed upstairs to the master bedroom. She threw her handbag onto a chair, stepped into the master bath, and took a shower. Amy stood under the water for a long time before stepping out into the cool air. She looked at her five foot seven inch frame in the mirror, her slender features, and petite breasts. She touched herself with a half hearted smile then took a robe that was hanging next to the sink and put it on.

Back down on the main level of the house, she took out a bottle of Jack Daniels and a highball glass and made her way back to the master bedroom. She poured a full glass and drank it quickly, then sat on the edge of the bed and broke into tears. "Dear God…what have I done?" She caught the image of her handbag on the chair in the corner of the bedroom where she had dropped it and removed the gun. She was still in tears as she staggered back over to the bed and flipped the chamber open to see five bullets not six. She poured another glass of whisky and drank it down fast. "I have to do this while I still have my nerve, or I will be lost forever." Her speech was slurring, and she laid down on the bed propped up by the throw pillows. Amy allowed the robe to fall open. She picked up the gun, slammed the cylinder closed, cocked it, pressed the barrel to the roof of her mouth, and pulled the trigger.

The Eagle had Alan Holden and Clive Montgomery in the back of his truck. He also had a passenger. Joanna Fines sat silent in shock next to the Eagle as he turned into the drive of his underground lair and into the parking lot. He parked the truck, got out, and opened the passenger door. Joanna didn't move. She stared off into space. He picked her up in his huge arms and carried her into the house. Sara was sitting in the foyer when he came walking in. She didn't say a word but stood and walked over to him as he laid the girl on one of the sofas. "Shock?" she asked. The Eagle nodded. "I assume you have someone else?" The Eagle nodded, holding up two fingers. Sara walked down the hall and opened the operating rooms and lit them up. She set up IVs and other apparatus as the Eagle brought in his prey. "How long will they be out?" Sara asked as the Eagle stripped and then strapped Holden to one of the gurneys. "Maybe ten more minutes. I gave them a low dose sedative after I tased them." The Eagle walked out as Sara set an IV in Holden's left arm. The Eagle stripped and strapped Clive to the other gurney in the room next to Alan, and Sara set an IV for him as well. Sliding a steel table of instruments over to Sara, the Eagle asked her to prep them for use. He walked out to the couch where Joanna lay in a silent stare. He had a syringe in his hand and gave Joanna an injection then wrapped her in a robe and covered her with a blanket. Her eyes slowly closed. She never made eye contact with the Eagle at all.

The underground drive was already open when Jim and Randy turned into the Eagle's lair. Jim parked the car, and Randy got out as well as Jessica. Jim led the way. "Where are we?" Jessica asked. "The less you know the better." They walked in, and Jim could see a young girl laying on the couch. The Eagle walked out at that moment, and Jim asked, "Are we fuckin' collecting these kids now…what the fuck?" The Eagle told Jim to take Jessica to other quarters as Sara emerged from the operating rooms. She saw Randy right away and asked, "What is he doing here?" The Eagle ordered Strom to sit while he picked up Joanna and carried her, following Jim to one of the unoccupied guest houses. He laid Joanna on a bed and told him to remain with them until he called. Jim nodded with no words.

The Eagle walked back into the foyer where Sara and Randy sat together. She looked up at the Eagle, and Randy looked at Sara and said, "It's been a long time since we've spoken, Sara." She nodded. "Congratulations on your inheritance and your marriage." "Thank you, Randy. I'm sorry for your loss. I do feel that that is somehow going to be mitigated by my husband." She pointed in the direction of the Eagle, who stood towering over the two of them. "Follow me!" Randy did as instructed and was brought into an operating room. There was a nude man he did not recognize on a gurney. Alan was starting to rouse, and Randy asked, "Do I know this person?" The Eagle pointed at Alan Holden and said, "No…you are about to be introduced. Please remain silent." Holden opened his eyes to see the Eagle standing over him. It was cold, and he could see bright lights above as well as television monitors all around him. He turned his head and saw his body strapped to a gurney. When he realized he was nude, he started to scream.

The Eagle slapped him with the back of his gloved hand and said, "SILENCE!" Holden was spitting teeth and blood as the Eagle moved a steel tray next to his body. "You and I are going to have a talk, Mr. Holden. You are going to give me your full confession about the Hollywood serial killings." Holden's face was swelling when he said, "I don't know what you're talking about." The Eagle took a syringe off the table and injected some medication into Holden's IV. There were a few moments of silence then Holden became more animated and conversational. "Why am I here? What do you want from me?" The Eagle took a photograph from the table and showed it to Holden. "Do you recognize this girl?" Holden squinted. "Oh, yes…" he laughed, "my little Suzy Q." Randy jumped up. The Eagle heard him and without turning from Holden said, "Sit down, detective. You need to be patient. You will get your turn. You have my word," the Eagle said in a cool and monotone voice. "Your

Suzy Q, you say?" The Eagle had not removed the photo from Holden's sight. "Oh, yes…Clive picked her up and brought her to the house. We had a great shoot and then great sex. I left her to Clive after I had satisfied my lust for her body."

The Eagle put down the picture and asked, "Why did you leave her to Clive?" Holden was giggling and said, "Clive likes to be brutal on the flesh. I fuck them; he handles them when I'm finished, then we upload the images to our clients in kiddy porn land. You would be amazed at just how many people want to see kids getting fucked." Holden laughed and said, "It is quite profitable…a nice supplement to my 'adult' modeling business." Holden paused then looked at the Eagle and asked, "Who are you? Where am I?" The Eagle took a pair of copper cables and clamped them onto Holden's testicles, then took a pair of brass nails, and with all of his strength, drove them down into Holden's thighs. Strom heard the sound of metal on metal as the spikes passed through the man's flesh. Holden screamed as each testicle was pinched by the spring loaded cables. The Eagle answered as he finished wiring Holden up, "Who am I you ask? I'm known by several names. You might know me best by my nickname. I am the Iron Eagle."

Holden started screaming, first from what could only be name recognition, and, second, from the 110 volts of electricity passing through his scrotum and thighs. The Eagle turned to Randy and said, "Here is the man who sexually assaulted your daughter. Follow me, and I will introduce you to the man who killed her." Randy didn't make a sound as he watched Holden convulsing on the table as they left the room, then he asked, "You're not going to kill them, are you?" "No, Detective Strom. I will leave that to you." The Eagle called out to Sara and asked her to turn down the voltage on Mr. Holden. Randy saw Sara walking up the hall headed for the operating room as the Eagle opened the door across the hall to where Clive Montgomery laid immobile and very alert.

"Mr. Montgomery, allow me to introduce myself. I am the Iron Eagle, and the man behind me is the father of Suzy Strom…you remember that name, don't you?" Clive didn't move or make a sound; he just stared at the Eagle dressed in all black, his dead eyes staring into his soul. Randy walked over next to the table and saw that there was a steel piece of cable on a metal tray next to it. He picked it up with both hands and began to beat Clive on the genitals, screaming as he did, "You sick son of a bitch. You killed my baby, and you tortured and mutilated my daughter." Montgomery was now screaming and pleading with each blow of the half inch steel cable. The Eagle grabbed Randy's arm and said, "Enough. Mr. Montgomery has a confession to make…don't you, Mr. Montgomery?" He was crying on the gurney as the Eagle injected him with the same clear liquid he had given to Holden. The Eagle pointed a remote at a wall, and the monitors came to life.

Sara came into the room and said, "It's half past nine. I assume this will be one of your all nighters?" The Eagle nodded. "Will you need me right away, or can I get some dinner?" "Thank you for your help. Please go eat. Detective Strom and I are going to spend some time with both of these gentlemen. I will call you when I am ready to dispatch them." Sara smiled and left the room. Strom looked at the Eagle and asked, "Sara is a part of this?" The Eagle answered, "She wasn't always, but she has developed a taste for it. It's quite convenient having a medical doctor on hand to assist. She does good work at keeping my prey alive." Strom looked on, and he was breathing heavy. "You're going to kill me, aren't you, John?" The Eagle reached his hands behind his head and removed his mask. "All this time. It's been you all along. You are the Iron Eagle. You're extracting justice for the victims and their families," Strom said, taking deep heavy breaths of sheer panic. "I see you know my work." He said it as he clamped off Montgomery's testicles and sent 110 volts through his body.

He didn't look at Randy, just lowered the voltage. "You're going to want to talk to me, Mr. Montgomery. It will make your death faster. How many people have you killed?" The medication was starting to take effect, and once Clive started talking there was nothing that was going to stop him. It was half past eleven when he finished his confession, and when he was done, Randy sat down in a corner of the room with tears running down his face. The Eagle asked, "All of these victims were found by Alan Holden?" He nodded and said, "Alan got the sex while I got the footage, and then he gave them to me to enjoy." The Eagle pressed his right arm into Clive's chest, and Randy could hear the man's ribs snapping like twigs. Once released, his breathing was labored, and he was barely able to speak. "I did what Alan told me to do. Did I enjoy it? Yes. Would I do it again?" A smile grew across his weak face. "Absolutely!"

The Eagle handed Randy his field knife and said, "Kill him as you see fit." The Eagle stepped back from the table as Randy butchered Clive. Blood was flying as Randy tempered his rage with each slash of the blade. At first, Clive attempted to scream, but those screams were literally drowned out by the blood pooling in his chest and abdomen. Randy stepped away from Montgomery's bloody body, and the knife hit the floor as he looked at what he had done. Clive's body was mutilated, yet he was still breathing, taking slow, shallow breaths. The Eagle picked up the field knife and asked, "Are you satisfied, Randy? Should I dispatch Mr. Montgomery?" Randy had moved back to a far wall away from the scene. He was shuddering as the Eagle spoke. He didn't make a move or give an answer. The Eagle took the knife and opened Clive's chest cavity. He used a bone saw to split his sternum and a rib spreader to open his chest. Clive was in shock as the Eagle finished the work of opening his chest and lifting his heart so he could see it. "Well, Mr. Montgomery, Mr. Strom has made quite a mess of you and my operating room." He held Clive's heart in his hands and pulled it up high enough that Randy could see it beating. "I suppose it's time to kill you now. I have Alan Holden to deal with." And with those words the Eagle gripped Clive's aorta and twisted it until it popped like a balloon in his chest, sending what little blood that was left in his body down into his chest cavity. Randy watched as Clive's pupil's dilated, and the Eagle called to Sara to pronounce Mr. Montgomery's death. The Eagle turned to Randy and said, "Well...shall we deal with Mr. Holden?"

CHAPTER TWELVE

"It's not a goddamn suicide note, you dumb mother fucker. It's a shopping list!"

Jim was sitting with the two girls when one of his lead detectives called. He listened as Jessica looked on, and Joanna remained asleep. He hung up the line and called John's cell phone. "Swenson." John listened intently, all the while looking at Randy, who had his back pressed hard against the wall of the operating room where Clive Montgomery's body remained. John hung up the line, took a syringe from the steel table near the operating table and Clive's body, and stabbed it into Randy's thigh. As Randy sunk into unconsciousness, John asked, "What did you do to Terry Brady?" Randy was shaking his head as he passed out. John called to Sara and asked her to keep an eye on the two girls in the guest house. She asked if she could call Barbara for assistance, and he said yes as he walked toward the parking garage. Jim was standing next to his car when John walked out. He had a cigarette in his hand and was breathing out a puff of smoke when John got to the door of his truck. "This is going to be a fuckin' game changer, Mr. Eagle, a fuckin' game changer. The two men jumped into their vehicles, and Jim followed John through the tunnel to PCH.

Barbara got to Sara within minutes of the men leaving. She was sitting on the sun deck of the guest house that Jim and Barbara stayed in while they were recovering from the LA fires nearly two years earlier. Jessica was sitting on one of the deck chairs when Barb entered, and Joanna was asleep on the couch in the living room. "Did you inherit an instant family?" Barbara asked with a little laugh. "It sure as hell feels that way," Sara said. She looked over at Jessica and said, "No offense." "None taken." Barbara hadn't seen Jessica, and when she heard her voice she called her name then saw a pair of young feet on a recliner on the deck. Sara looked over at Barbara and asked, "Do you two know each other?" Barbara smiled and said, "Yea...Jim brought her home last night. It seems he's taken a shine to her." Barb looked at Jessica and asked, "What are you still doing with my husband?" Jessica sat staring into the darkness. She commented on the sound of the surf as she replied to Barbara. "I want to go back to my street corner, Mrs. O'Brian; it is the sheriff who has been holding me. From what I can gather thus far, the mug shot book that the sheriff gave me had two men that he was looking for in it. Now I'm just waiting for him to release me, and I will be on my way. I have clients that I need to see. I do have a living to make." Sara looked confused then asked Barbara, "How old is she?" Jessica answered, "Old enough to know better, and young enough not to care!" Barbara explained the situation with Jessica to Sara, who was appalled. "Prostitution is not a profession for anyone, especially a child." Jessica and Barbara looked at each other, and Jessica broke into laughter, as did Barbara.

"What's so damn funny?" Sara asked. Jessica stopped laughing and said, "That's easy for you to say, Dr. Swenson. You have options, and I'm a kid who's been on the streets for several years. I need a roof and food. I provide my clients with what they want, and in exchange they provide me with what I need. I'm in a profession, Doctor; the oldest profession in the world." Sara looked at her and said, "Don't you understand the risks not just to your health but physical safety risks?" "It's easy to assess the risks when you have a roof over your head and food to eat. I understand the risks. I insist on condoms with all of my clients, but there are those who want the natural experience, and I'm not in a position to get a reputation on the street as a condom-only hooker. I am on birth control; I get it from the free clinic on Hollywood Boulevard. I get HIV tests every month, and when a john I don't know wants sex without a condom, I try to get him off with oral sex with an over-exaggerated swallow. If they insist on penetration, then I insist on anal sex, so I don't have to even think about pregnancy. Even birth control is not a hundred percent guarantee, and I don't want no babies or abortions as a result of the johns I do." Sara sat looking at Jessica. She heard the words coming out of the young girl's mouth, but it was as if she were hearing them from someone twenty years older.

"Where the hell did Jim find her?" she asked Barbara. "On the street. He is protecting her from the Hollywood Killer, though I think that the Eagle has that under control from what Jim told me. Jessica stood up and walked barefoot over to the pool at the edge of the deck and stuck a toe in. "Ah…heated. May I swim?" Sara nodded, and Jessica took off her clothes and jumped into the water. Barbara walked back into the house and poured herself a scotch and called out to Sara. "First, do you want a drink? And second, why isn't the girl on the couch moving." Sara called back to her, "Yes, and the Eagle sedated her. She's in shock, and John and Jim haven't told me what they are going to do with her." Barbara came back with the drinks in her hands, looking at Joanna's legs and said, "I could think of a few things to do with a body like that!" Sara frowned. "I don't know her age for sure, but I know she is under eighteen." Barbara smiled and said, "Man, I remember being a teenager. I envy Jessica the freedom she has." Sara took a drink and said, "I don't. She is a smart girl. There have to be other options for her outside of the life she has on the streets." Barbara sat down next to Sara and said, "I've been in law enforcement my entire life, Sara. I've seen everything you can imagine. Given her background and what she has escaped, that kid…" Barbara pointed to Jessica swimming in the pool, "will be just fine. She just needs the right launching point, and she will grow up to be a fine citizen." Sara nodded her head as she sipped her drink. "Yea…but first someone needs to give her a hand up not a hand out." Barbara nodded as Jessica kept swimming.

Terry Brady's residence was lit up by police cruisers and sheriff's cars alike when Jim and John arrived on scene. John walked up to the front door before Jim could get there and asked who made the call. One of Jim's deputies pointed to a young man, shaking, crying, and sitting on a stool in a corner of the living room. He saw Jade leaning over the body of Terry Brady, and he walked up to see Terry laying on her back, eyes wide open, and a small entrance wound in her right cheek. There was blood and brain matter on the wall directly behind her, and John stepped in and asked Jade when she got on scene. She stood up and looked at John's towering figure as Jim walked up to the two of them. "I and my people arrived about ten minutes ago. Right now, this might be a suicide. We are looking for the weapon." John looked at Terry's facial expression and her dilated pupils, which were turning a pale shade of gray from the air and lack of moisture and said, "This is not a suicide. It's a homicide. The question is who killed her?" Jim was standing next to John without speaking. Jade looked at him and said, "For a loud mouth fuckin' sheriff, you are quiet for this type of crime scene." "Yea…I'm quiet, Jade. I'm quiet for the moment. Can you estimate a time of death?" She looked down at the meat thermometer that was jammed into Terry's liver. "With a body temp of eighty six degrees based on the liver and the rate of rig in the body tissue, she's been dead less than twelve hours. I would estimate she died between three and six p.m. yesterday. It would be yesterday, right?" She looked at her PDA, which showed the time to be twelve forty-five a.m. "Yea, yesterday. My biological clock is off. She hasn't been dead very long. Why?" Jim was shaking his head. "Because that means the guy that we would nail for killing her ain't the fuckin' guy. We've got another killer." He said it looking at John who was looking over at the crying guy sitting on the stool.

John walked over to him and introduced himself. "My name is Special Agent John Swenson, FBI, and you are?" The young man shook hard and said, "Matthew… um….Matthew Hendricks. I'm Ms. Brady's personal assistant." "Did you find her?" He nodded. "What time?" He had a dazed look in his eyes. "Um…I was going home for the night. I hadn't heard from Ms. Brady all day. I had called her cell phone a few times, but there had been no answer. I was worried about her, so I stopped to check on her." Jim walked over and joined them. "What time did you show up here?" John asked. "…um … before dark. Probably six thirty." Jim asked, "Did you touch her body?" "I checked for a pulse, but there was none. So I called 911." Jim looked back at Brady's body then at Matthew and said, "The question I'm about to ask you is very important…was Ms. Brady warm to your touch when you found her?" There was a moment's pause, and he nodded his head. "Yea…she wasn't really, really warm, but she was warm enough for me to think that she might still be alive; after I called 911, I saw the blood behind her and realized that she had been shot." John asked, "You were one of the closest people to Ms. Brady. Was she depressed?" He looked at John and Jim like they had three heads. "Why would she be depressed? What possible reason could she have for being depressed? Oh, let's see. Her lover was just murdered, and the last words that they shared were not pleasant." John asked, "In what way? What was said?"

Matthew cleared his throat. "Um…they were fighting. Terry was yelling at Hillary because she had lied about the Strom girl in an article she released. She was angry with her. After the exchange, Hillary stormed out of the office, and that was the last time anyone saw her alive, including Terry. If I had a fight with my lover, and then he died before I could say I'm sorry, I would be depressed." John nodded slowly and waved Jim over toward him. As Jim was walking over, one of his detectives called out to him and said, "We have a note!" They went into the kitchen where the detective was holding a piece of paper in his gloved hand. Jim took a pair of gloves from one of his other officers, put them on, and took the note from the detective's hand. John was looking over his shoulder reading it. Jim got an angry look on his face and yelled, "It's not a goddamn suicide note, you dumb mother fucker. It's a shopping list!" His voice boomed off the walls of the kitchen. "Has anyone found the weapon…anyone, anyone at all?" His question was met with silence. "WELL, PEOPLE, IF THIS IS A SUICIDE THERE WOULD NOT ONLY BE A NOTE BUT ALSO THE GODDAMN GUN THAT BLEW HER FUCKIN' HEAD OFF!" "There's no weapon, Sheriff," one of his investigators said in a soft tone. "Did everyone hear that? There's no fuckin' gun. Guess what? That makes this a homicide scene, so stop looking for suicide notes and start looking for evidence."

John walked back to the body and Jade, who was back on her knees combing the scene around Terry's body. "It's not a suicide!" John said. Jade lifted a throw pillow that was on the floor next to Terry's head and said, "No shit, Sherlock…the killer muffled the gunshot with this." One of her people brought over an evidence bag, and John walked back to the front door where Jim joined him. "This one is baffling. Randy has been with us since four. He has an airtight alibi for Brady's murder. We have another killer." John was scratching his head as Jim pulled a cigarette out of his top left pocket and put it in his mouth while walking out of the house. He lit it and said, "Once again…can't get anything by you. Randy may not be the killer, but I have a very good hunch that he knows who the killer is." John looked around. The neighborhood was quiet, and the house was set way back off the street. John started walking down the long driveway when he noticed a cluster of neighbors at the end of the drive surrounded by media. There were several news crews interviewing people. He walked on as Jim stood under an oak tree smoking his cigarette. John had his FBI windbreaker on as he approached, and he looked on as the media paid no attention.

He looked around and was about to walk back to the house when he saw an older man with a cane motioning to him out of the lights. He walked over to him, and the old man said, "I saw the killer!" John leaned down to look in the old man's eyes and said, "Tell me." "Well…I saw a little foreign car, a Toyota or a Honda SUV, pull in the drive at about three forty-five yesterday afternoon. Two women got out; the driver I didn't recognize, but the passenger was Terry Brady. I saw them walk into the house and about ten or fifteen minutes later, I saw the woman driver run out and jump into her SUV and speed off." "Give me a description of her." "She was thin. Short black hair. She was dressed in a black pant suit like she had been in an important business meeting or something." "What color was the vehicle?" The old man was able to give John enough of a description and a partial plate number that he could run. John thanked him and went to walk away when he heard the old man say, "No problem. That's what they get for defying God's laws, those lesbians. They flaunted their defiance of God's law in his face, and God smote them."

John went back to his truck and called in the information. There were a few moments of silence on the radio when the dispatcher came back with only three matches for the license plate in the State of California. Dispatch sent over the information to John's computer. It took him only seconds, and he called out to Jim, "I think I have Ms. Brady's killer." Jim walked over, and John showed him his computer screen. Jim's face lit up. "No fuckin' shit…it makes perfect sense. We have an address. Let's pay a visit." Jim got in his car, and John took off for the 101 Freeway, Woodland Hills in the San Fernando Valley, and the home of Randy and Amy Strom.

CHAPTER THIRTEEN

*"It hurts, huh? You son of a
bitch...too fuckin' bad."*

Jessica went off to bed, and Sara checked on Joanna, who was sleeping soundly, though drugged. She and Barbara had been talking to each other on the deck when Sara heard a voice call out. She walked back to the operating room, and Randy Strom was standing in the middle of the room looking around confused. He was not restrained, and Sara was taken by surprise. Alan Holden was moaning on the operating room table next to Strom, and Randy looked at Sara and said, "You're a doctor, right?" She nodded. He said, "I want to kill this fucker, but I need help. I can't do it like I did with the other guy. Sara walked slowly toward Strom while speaking, "It's better if you wait for the Eagle before you do anything else. This is his realm." Randy made a wild move toward Sara, but she was able to dodge him but not before being thrown against the wall of the operating room. Randy had lost his balance as he was still under the influence of the sedative. It was obvious to Sara that he was seeing double, and she reached over to one of the steel tables and grabbed a syringe. She uncapped it and put it behind her back. Randy started screaming at her that he wanted Holden dead. He was going on and on about the fact that the Iron Eagle was John Swenson, and how he has been able to move in law enforcement with immunity without anyone knowing who he is.

Strom yelled out, "John Swenson is the Iron fuckin' Eagle. Now, I have to tell you, Mrs. Swenson, I didn't see that one coming." He was weaving from side to side as he walked toward Sara. "I bet the Iron Eagle would be devastated if his beautiful wife were killed brutally like my little Suzy was. I bet the Iron fuckin' Eagle would avenge your death. Fuckin' Swenson..." Randy put his fingers to his mouth, still staggering in Sara's direction. "Can I tell you a secret? Swenson's wife was murdered nearly fifteen years ago. The fucker never knew it, but I had the guy in custody who killed his wife ...I did, I had him." Sara started to get upset and said, "That's not true. You have no idea who killed my husband's late wife. You're lying!" Strom was still swaying back and forth, and he lunged for Sara, who moved out of the way, leaving Strom to hit the wall and fall onto a tray of instruments. He grabbed for the table and ended up with a scalpel embedded in his left hand. He howled and pulled it out and pointed it at Sara, who was now near the entrance to the room. Holden was moaning, trying to speak, and Strom yelled at him and pointed the scalpel in his direction. "I will deal with you in a second. I need to inflict more pain on your captor by killing his wife."

Strom turned back toward Sara and said, "You don't believe that I know who killed Amber Swenson? I was a patrol officer back in those days, and I saw a guy running out from behind the House of Pancakes. He darted in front of my cruiser. I grazed him with the front of my car, but he was only dazed and unhurt. I grabbed him and cuffed him. I took him back to where he had run out from in order to beat some sense into him. I kicked him in the stomach, and he rolled over on his side. I kicked him again, and then I saw the dumpster lid was open. I looked in and there was a dead nude blond. I heard the back door to the restaurant opening, so I grabbed the guy and drug him to my patrol car. I put him in the back and got in and drove off." Sara started crying hysterically. "No...that's a lie. You couldn't have known, and if you did why wouldn't you have taken him to the station?" Strom started laughing hysterically and said, "Because Walter Cruthers made me an offer I couldn't refuse. He made me a millionaire that day. He also pulled strings over the next six months to get me promoted to detective."

Sara was now in hysterics, and her own tears were clouding her ability to see Strom. He lurched forward and grabbed her by the throat, but she didn't fall. Instead, he felt another powerful arm grab him by the throat, and he felt a sharp pain in the side of his neck. Barbara had heard everything and had grabbed the syringe out of Sara's hysterical hand. She drove the needle deep into Strom's neck and held him as he hit the floor. She took Sara in her arms and helped to get her to a stool in the operating room. Barbara looked around and saw Holden on the gurney and Strom now asleep on the floor. She walked over to Holden and said, "You raped and killed children, you piece of shit, then you sold the videos on the Internet." She was standing over Holden as Sara looked on. "I know all about what you have done, Mr. Holden. My husband, Sheriff Jim O'Brian, told me all about it. You fucked up though. You left one of those kids alive, and she led the Iron Eagle and my husband to you and your boy toy. I have a feeling that the Iron Eagle is going to have more interest in Mr. Strom over there than you, so I'm going to do him a favor and get rid of you once and for all."

Barbara looked around the room and saw a large piece of equipment covered in a tan tarp. She pulled the tarp off, revealing an industrial meat grinder and a cherry picker. She walked over to Holden and released his restraints then bound his hands with a leather strap that she found hanging off the meat grinder. The grinder was all set up and plugged in. The cherry picker was on wheels, and she rolled it over to Holden and placed the steel hook, which hung from the picker, through the leather straps and pushed a button on the unit. Holden's nude body began to lift off the bed. He screamed as his arms were stretched and strained above his head as the unit lifted him higher into the air. "It hurts, huh? You son of a bitch…too fuckin' bad." Sara was staring at Barbara as she rolled the picker over to the grinder, putting Holden's body over the hopper. She locked the wheels down on the picker, pulled two stainless steel meat trays from the other side of the wall, and placed one in front of the feeder and the other next to the boning shoot.

"My father was a butcher in my home country of Ireland; Dublin, to be exact. I worked in his shop from the time I was a wee girl until I moved to the United States to go to college. I'm sure the Iron Eagle won't mind me putting you though this fine piece of equipment. He keeps it very, very clean." Barbara walked over to the control panel and turned it on. The blades began to churn beneath Holden's feet, and she called out to Sara and said, "Get out of here. You don't want to see and hear what's about to happen to this child raping killing piece of garbage." Sara stood up and walked over and stood next to Barbara and said, "Send him to hell!" Barbara pushed the auto lower button on the cherry picker, and Holden was lowered into the meat grinding and cutting blades at the slowest possible speed. Holden's screams were blood curdling, and she stopped the unit just above Holden's thighs while she and Sara strapped Strom to the gurney and turned it so he had a view of what was happening to Holden.

Sara injected Strom with a high dose of stimulant, and he awoke with a start, looking around at where he was. He tried to move but couldn't. Sara whispered into his ear, "I wanted you to be conscious for this, Detective Strom. I want you to see what the Iron Eagle is going to do to you when I tell him that you let Amber Lynn Swenson's killer go free. She was my best friend, detective." Barbara hit the start switch again, and Holden began to lower into the meat grinder. Strom screamed as he watched Holden with his arms over his head entering the feeder of the grinder whole, and his body emerging with the consistency of hamburger. The two men were screaming; Holden, as the machine devoured his body, and Strom, watching in horror at the fate that most likely awaited him.

Jim and John arrived at the Strom home in Woodland Hills just before three a.m. The house was actually a mansion nestled at the end of a cul-de-sac on Canyonwood Drive. There was a great deal of land around it and nothing but views out over the San Fernando Valley and the Agoura Hills behind it. John and Jim approached the home and knocked on the front door, which opened to their knock. The two looked at each other, drew their weapons, and entered the house. The house was so large and well lit that they expected to scare Amy Strom as she roamed the house, but everything was silent. They cleared the lower floors and proceeded up the stairs to the second level. Jim commented that one of these two must be loaded. He whispered to John, "Do you have any idea how much a home like this costs in a neighborhood like this? Millions, mother fucker, millions of mother fuckin' dollars." The second floor was dark unlike the lower level. They passed Suzy's room where they had searched early in the investigation. They crossed a huge open air loft and looked down into the lower level floor plan. It was an impressive view. There was a light on at the far end of the hall, and John and Jim each took a side then entered the room sweeping their guns as they moved. Jim walked into a well lit room as John moved in the other direction. Jim cleared the master bathroom and walked into the foyer of the master bedroom where he saw John standing with his gun at his side.

Jim looked over to see what was left of Amy Strom's head splattered on the wall behind the bed. John drew a pair of gloves out of his pocket, put them on, and gave Jim a pair. Jim turned on the lights in the room to reveal the horror of what had happened. John looked down to see that Amy's robe was open. She was nude; there was a .357 Magnum in her right hand on the bed next to her. There was a half consumed bottle of Jack Daniels and a half full glass tumbler. Jim looked at John and said, "There won't be a suicide note." John nodded as he took his phone off his belt and called for backup and his crime scene team.

Jade Morgan and her team were on scene before anyone else. She walked into the bedroom and took one look at Amy and asked, "Who found her?" Jim and John told her it was them. "What the fuck, guys? Do you know her?" Jim snorted, and John half laughed. John told her that they had met at her daughter's funeral the day before. Jade remembered the Strom girl and shook her head as she started to process the scene. She looked at John and asked, "Is this a crime scene?" He looked at Jim and then at Jade and said, "Yes and no. This is a suicide, but run the bullet found in the Brady homicide through ballistics, and you will get a match to the .357 in the cold dead hand of Amy Strom." Jade was picking up skull fragments and bagging them as the other teams arrived on scene, and she asked, "Amy Strom killed Terry Brady?" Both men nodded. "But why? How the hell would they know each other?" John said, "It will all come out in the report." They went to leave the room when Jade asked, "Who is going to let the husband know?" John raised his hand and said, "I'll take care of it. It's the least I can do for him. He's been through enough." With that, they left. Once outside, Jim lit a cigarette and asked, "So, back to the Iron Eagle?" John sighed and nodded as they both got into their cars and headed back to Malibu.

CHAPTER FOURTEEN

*"Barbara looked down at the ground and
said, "I already dealt with that child killer."*

It was nearing dawn when John pulled into the underground parking of the Eagle's lair. Jim was not far behind him, and when Jim got out of his car John asked, "Aren't you going to go home to your wife?" Jim took out a smoke and clinched it between his teeth and said, "I'd love to, but she left me a message that she's here with Sara. Remember, dipshit? You told Sara it was okay to have Barbara over when we left?" John nodded, and they walked into the foyer of the room to see Barbara and Sara sitting alone on the deck overlooking the sea. "Where are the girls?" Jim asked. "Jessica is asleep in the far bedroom, and Sara sedated the other girl who is asleep in the other room. "She needs to be taken to the hospital." John looked at Sara who nodded, stood up, and grabbed a hold of John with everything she had. He hugged her back. When he realized by her grip that her hug was not a hug of joy, he pulled her away to look into her eyes. "What?" She didn't say a word. She just started weeping. John looked at Barbara and asked, "What has gone on here since we left?" Barbara walked down the hall to the operating room where the door was closed. John followed her, and Jim stayed behind with Sara.

Barbara took John's hand and said, "After you left, Sara and I had a nice conversation with Jessica, the young lady that made it possible for you to find the animals that were killing the kids. Strom came to after you left, and he wasn't restrained. He tried to attack Sara, and I put him down with an injection. John moved toward the door in anger, but Barbara stopped him. "Strom was talking gibberish at first, but in the end he bragged that he knew who killed Amber. He confessed that he was a patrol officer back then, and that Amber's killer ran out in front of his cruiser. Strom found out that the guy he hit had killed your late wife. Cruthers paid him off to keep quiet. He claimed that Cruthers pulled strings to get him promoted to detective and made his lot in life much better." John stood silent for a long time before he said anything. "I have to deal with Holden, then I will deal with Strom."

Barbara looked down at the ground and said, "I already dealt with that child killer." John looked down at Barbara and asked, "What did you do to him?" "My father was a butcher in Dublin. I worked in his shop from the time I was little. I found your meat grinder, and I made hamburger out of him. I also let Strom watch and told him it was most likely his fate. I have cleaned the hopper and the blades. I put Holden's remains in the operating room with the body of his partner. I didn't know how you would want to dispose of them. I hope you're not angry with me. I wasn't going to let that son of a bitch, Strom, hurt Sara, and I'm sorry, but after all that Jim told me of what Holden has done, mine was a crime of passion. I wanted to see him suffer." John leaned down and took Barbara in his huge arms and hugged her. She disappeared into his hold, and he felt her body begin to shake as the tears were able to come, and he held her tight to comfort her. He whispered into her ear, "Thank you for protecting Sara. Now leave me to deal with Strom." He released her, and she got her composure and walked out to where Jim and Sara were waiting for her.

The Iron Eagle opened the door to the operating room where Randy Strom was strapped to a gurney. Strom looked over and saw him enter but said nothing. The Eagle grabbed a stool from a corner of the room and pulled it over next to Strom's head. The Eagle drew a deep breath and said softly, "Your wife is dead!" Randy looked at him and started screaming, "What the fuck did you do? She didn't do anything to you! Why the hell would you hurt her?" "I didn't hurt her. Jim O'Brian and I found her with a self-inflicted gunshot wound to the head. She only did that after she took Terry Brady back to her residence and shot her in the head. The pieces have been coming together over the past several hours. We were able to track a taxi service that your wife used from a storage facility that you two have in your name to your home. We have an eyewitness who saw your wife drive up with Ms. Brady in her car and go into Ms. Brady's home. She left in a hurry right about the time you were meeting with me and Jim at my office. Now, I'm going to go out on a limb here and guess that you abducted Ms. Brady two nights ago after you killed Hillary Sums. You didn't want to kill her right away; you took her to your storage unit until you could figure out what you were going to do with her.

"I figure your wife learned of what you did after the funeral and tried to talk you out of it. She then went to the storage facility where she talked Brady into letting you off the hook and even took her out of there. Those facilities have excellent security cameras, so I'm pretty sure it's all on tape. The problem was your wife, being a psychologist, had second thoughts when she dropped off Terry Brady and killed her instead because she was a newswoman. She knew that what you did to Brady would get out sooner or later, so to protect you, Amy killed her. Once she understood what she had done, having lost her daughter and knowing eventually she would lose you, too, she felt an overwhelming guilt that you can't understand and took her own life." Randy was silent. "You really don't care, do you Randy? Your wife, your daughter? Your self-righteous attitude through all of this is just a front." Silence met the question. "You knew all of these years who killed my wife, and you let him go. You cost dozens of women and children their lives at the cruel and sadistic hands of Walter Cruthers. You could have stopped all of it. It was your job. It is what you were sworn to do." Silence met the calm quiet voice of the Eagle.

The Eagle stood up and grabbed a leather strap off the grinder and released Strom's hands. He tried to fight, but the Eagle smashed in his teeth. Once he had him restrained by the wrists, the Eagle pulled over the dental unit he had added to his torture collection some years ago, and with one hand, pinned Strom to the gurney, and with the other, drilled into Strom's face. He drilled tooth after tooth. He would stop every few minutes to spray ice water into the gaping holes in Strom's face and teeth. The screams of agony were held between the walls of the operating room. The Eagle continued until all of Strom's teeth had been drilled out and all of the nerves exposed. He slapped Strom across the face, knocking out some loosened teeth, then took ice from a cooler he had in the room and forced it into Strom's mouth. Strom's screams were constant as he writhed on the gurney.

The Eagle pulled a pair of copper cables from a battery charger and laid them on Strom's chest. He ripped the clothes from his body, grabbed a scalpel and the man's penis, and removed it, sending arterial spray in all directions. The Eagle grabbed his seal, and the white hot symbol of the Eagle glowed as he pressed it in into Strom's crotch, cauterizing the wound. He snapped the copper clips onto Strom's testicles and turned the unit to full power. Strom seized against the current. The Eagle raised and lowered the current for over a half hour as Strom resisted the current flowing through his groin. Then the Eagle ripped the clamps off, opening the skin of Strom's scrotum, spilling his testicles onto the table. He grabbed each one and ripped them out by the root. When Strom passed out, the Eagle woke him with a high power stimulant injection, and his pain intensified.

"Death…Oh God! Please kill me!" Strom managed to stutter, but the Eagle persisted until there was nothing left of Strom's flesh but bloodied unrecognizable meat. Emasculated, Strom laid still. The Eagle moved the cherry picker over, placed the hook between Strom's hands, slowly raised his bloodied body, and moved him over to the grinder. He released the lock on the picker and started the meat grinder then looked Strom in the eye. He set the machine to its slowest possible speed and walked out, but not before saying, "MAY GOD NOT HAVE MERCY ON YOUR SOUL!"

Strom's screams were drowned out as the Eagle closed the operating room door behind him. He walked to the back of the hall and took Holden and Montgomery's remains out to the incinerator. When Strom's body had been consumed, the Eagle did the same with it. He spent another hour cleaning both operating rooms and sanitizing them. No one would know that they had ever had inhabitants. When the Eagle had finished his duties, he walked out to where Sara, Barbara, and Jim were sitting in the foyer waiting area. John sat down, winded, and said, "Jim, you need to take the girl from Holden's to the hospital, then you know what to do with his home and Holly Bachman." He nodded. "What about Jessica?" Barbara asked. Sara said, "Send her here to the main house. I'm going to make sure she has an opportunity to get off the streets." With that everyone departed, and John and Sara stood alone looking out at the sea after sunrise with their arms around each other, neither saying a word.

CHAPTER FIFTEEN

"The Eagle will do what he can to stop the carnage in this
city until one day he, too, might just ... disappear."

Holly Bachman was fast asleep when she heard the screeching sound of car tires outside her bedroom window. She didn't get the chance to get out of bed before there was pounding on her front door and the call of, "Sheriff's Department. Open up." She grabbed a robe and opened the front door. She was grabbed by two SWAT officers, taken off the property, and placed into the back of a squad car. The Eagle had made an anonymous 911 call that he routed through the phone lines to appear to come from Holden's residence. Jim 'O'Brian stood with his SWAT team and bomb squad as they shouted out orders but received no response. Jim called in the FBI, and John arrived on scene at eight thirty a.m., a half hour after Jim and his men. News and police choppers hovered over the residence. The Getty Center had been evacuated as had four blocks around Holden's home. Holly was screaming for Holden from the back of a patrol car. It was noon before John and Jim's teams cleared the scene, and as they moved from house to house and building to building, the more complete the picture of Holden and Montgomery's depravity became.

When the scene had finally been cleared, an APB was issued for the men, and Jim and John's men were hauling out computer systems and projectors as well as bag after bag of evidence. The torture table used by Montgomery to kill his young victims was being evaluated by Jade and her team. Over the next several days, twenty-three bodies were unearthed on Holden's property, all of them between thirteen and eighteen. Jade held a news conference with Jim letting the media know of the gruesome discovery, and that it was quite likely that the remains found at the house would never be identified. John held a news conference later to let the media know that they were seeking Holden and Montgomery, and that they were suspected of being the Hollywood Killers.

When John had finished his news conference, Jim walked up to him, and the two men walked the scene. They moved off out of the camera's eye and stood in the shadow of the Getty Center, and Jim said, "You know that this is going to become the next big tourist attraction." John nodded, looking out over the large plot of land that also overlooked the 405 Freeway between Skirball Center Drive and Sunset Boulevard. John laughed and said, "The neighbors are going to love us. We just created the second biggest attraction next to The Getty, quite literally. Narrow streets and winding roads will make living in this area a nightmare. I can see the tour buses now." Jim let out a howl of laughter and said, "You're becoming as jaded a fuck as I am. Too bad no one will know what happened to the Hollywood Killers. They are going to be the stuff of legends like the Zodiac Killer. Kill for a brief time, disappear, then become a legend. No more victims, no more information, a city left paralyzed with fear without answers or closure."

John was staring off into the distance and said, "Yea...but people have short memories. If there is one thing I have learned in my years of police work, it's that this is a city that always forgets the past and is doomed to repeat it." Jim lit a cigarette, took a few drags, and said, "Yep...and what are they going to do when the Iron fuckin' Eagle isn't here to protect them?" John took a deep breath and turned to Jim and said, "That's not his problem, now is it? The Eagle will do what he can to stop the carnage in this city until one day he, too, might just ... disappear." Jim got a huge smile as they heard Jade calling out to them from down near the end of the property line. The two men went to meet with her and to discuss what should happen to the scene.

Barbara had just dropped Jessica off with Sara and was back at the house getting ready to take a shower for work when her cell phone rang. She grabbed it thinking it was Jim, but the voice on the other end of the line caught her off guard. "Hi, Barbara, it's Gail Hoffman." Barbara smiled and asked, "Gail, sweetheart, to what do I owe the honor of your call?" There was a moment of hesitation, and Gail said, "Steve and I are coming out to LA in the next couple of days, and I know it would mean the world to Steve to see Jim." Barbara got a confused look on her face and asked, "While I'm quite certain that Jim will be very happy to see Steve, why are you calling me about an upcoming trip? Why doesn't Steve call Jim or John?" Gail paused for a second and said, "Our trip is a social visit not related to Steve's duties, and I wanted to see what accommodations are like out there now. As you know Steve lost the house in the valley in the fires, and he took the insurance money instead of rebuilding." "Well, the city has been recovering slowly. Most of the hotels downtown are operating again, and, of course, the closer you push toward the beach the more amenities there are." Barbara stopped mid sentence and asked, "This is not just a social call, is it Gail?" There were a few moments of silence and Barbara heard Gail take a deep breath. "No."

"What's going on Gail? Why are you calling me?" "I was hoping we could talk in person when Steve and I get into LA." "When are you arriving?" "Tomorrow morning. The Bureau set us up in the Water Front Hotel in Santa Monica." Barbara stalled for a few seconds and then asked, "Is Steve going to call John or Jim to let them know you're coming out?" There was silence. "Gail?" Barbara heard a sniffle on the line, and she could tell that Gail was crying. "No...Steve wants to make it a surprise." "Uh huh, and you're calling me to give me a heads up that you're coming?" "Yes." Barbara was standing in the bathroom taking off her clothes for the shower. "And you don't want to talk to me on the phone about the reason for the visit?" "I would rather speak to you in person." Barbara agreed. Gail gave her the check in time at the hotel for the following afternoon, and Barbara put it into her PDA. She hung up the line and showered and took off for work. She had her cell phone in her hand as she walked into the federal court house headed for her office with Jim's number open in her contacts. She was agonizing about whether to call Jim or not. She was just getting ready to make the call when she got orders that there was unrest with several prisoners in detention. Barbara clipped the phone to her belt and decided she would speak to Jim after work and headed for prisoner holding.

Holly Bachman was sitting in an all too familiar place — the interrogation room at FBI headquarters. John was sitting across from her, and he was asking her about the things that Alan Holden and Clive Montgomery had been doing, grilling her on what she knew. "Special Agent Swenson, I'm telling you I know very little about what Alan and Clive did in their business. When Alan took me in, he called me his 'pet project,' that's all." John was sitting across the table from her in a short sleeve FBI polo shirt and blue jeans, staring at her with a look of disbelief. "I hope you can understand my skepticism. You lived under his roof. You two were lovers. You can see why it is a little hard for me to believe that you knew nothing." Holly got teary eyed and said, "I only slept with Alan once and that was last week. He never touched me before then, and I wanted it." "Did he take pictures or video of you having sex?" She got a horrified look on her face. "Of course not. What we shared was true love. I wanted him to be my first, and he was. It was sensual and loving."

John leaned back in his chair. "Was there ever any talk of you having sex with anyone other than Holden?" Holly shuddered and said, "The night before the sheriff came to the house we had been out to dinner with Clive, and Alan did say that he wanted me and him and Clive to have a threesome. I don't know what that is, but he told me I would like it." "But that never happened?" "No...the last time I saw Alan he was tucking me into bed after we talked about it, and that was it." John stood up and said, "Well, it is all over the media, and it is obvious to me that you have not seen the news, so I might as well be the one to tell you this. Alan Holden and Clive Montgomery were the Hollywood Killers." Holly's face took on a look of horror. "No...that's impossible. I was with Alan almost nonstop. There is no way." John nodded and explained everything. When he finished, Holly threw up in a trash can in the interrogation room, and John left her to Anita Bandon to deal with.

He went back to his office, and the message light on his office phone was blinking. He picked it up and retrieved a message from Steve Hoffman. *"Hey, John, it's Steve. I hope my message finds you well. I've heard that there is no lack of excitement out there. Listen, I'm taking a few weeks of vacation, and I'm coming back to LA. I wanted to see if you will have some time to talk when I'm out. You don't need to call me back. Gail and I will be staying at the Water Front Hotel in Santa Monica. I will give you a call when we get in."* John hung up the phone and called Jim.

"Have you received any calls from Steve?" "Nope. Not that I know of. Why?" "I just got a message on my office line saying he's coming to LA tomorrow with Gail, and he wants to hook up." There were a few moments of silence, and Jim asked, "Is he coming out here on FBI business?" "No...he said he's coming out for vacation. He's staying at the Water Front Hotel and wants to hook up when he gets in tomorrow." "Huh...what the fuck? I wonder why he hasn't called me," Jim asked, but John had no reply. John asked if he and Barbara were meeting him and Sara for dinner, and he told him yes. "Well, then let's talk about it more then. I need to get over to Northridge Hospital and see what the kid we saved from Holden knows and, most importantly, remembers." Jim laughed and said, "Yea...I doubt that she is going to remember you as her black angel like Karen Barstow did." John laughed. "That reminds me. I need to give Karen a call. I had promised that she could bring some of her friends over to the house for a pool party nearly a month ago, and I haven't followed through on that." Jim let out a chuckle and told him he would call him later if there was anything new on the case. John hung up and called Sara to make sure that she had the girl at the hospital, and he took off for Northridge.

Joanna Fines was lying in a hospital bed, still catatonic, staring off into space. Sara was talking to one of her staff who had worked her up for everything and found nothing physically wrong with her. Sara had called the head of psychiatry, Ted Ringfield, who spent several hours with Joanna, and he was as baffled as the next person. "I don't know what to tell you, Sara. The girl has been shocked beyond the ability to communicate; there is the very real chance that she will never come out of it." Sara shook her head as Ted walked off, and she saw John walking the hallway toward her. "Well?" he asked. "Nothing...she has said nothing...there's nothing physically wrong with her, honey...I even had Ted come down and check her out. He feels she has been shocked beyond the ability to communicate, and she could quite likely remain that way forever."

John asked if he could see her; Sara nodded and told him she had to do some rounds and would come back in a bit. John walked into Joanna's room where she just lay on the bed staring at a wall. He moved a chair from a corner of the room and sat down in front of her face. John looked into her eyes and said, "You are safe. I know that you have been exposed to some very scary stuff, but you weren't raped or beaten. I want to help you, but you have to help me. We don't even know your name...there could be someone looking for you, and no one will find you unless you talk to me." She blinked but didn't make a move. John leaned in and whispered into her ear, "They are dead...the men who took you and who hurt you are dead!" He sat back in his chair, but it seemed to have no effect.

He stood up from the chair and started to move it when he heard Joanna say something. He leaned down to look in her eyes, and she made eye contact with him. "What's your name?" She blinked a couple of times fast as if waking up and said, "Joanna...Joanna Fines." John put his hand on her shoulders, and she started screaming and jerked away from him. Two nurses ran into the room to sedate her, but he told them not to. "Leave her be...she needs to let it out." She had turned onto her back screaming as John pulled out his tablet and typed her name into the NCIC database. Ten seconds later, he had a missing persons report for a Joanna Fines from Hollywood, who was last seen on Hollywood Boulevard. Her mother had reported the girl missing two and a half days ago. Joanna was still screaming, and

John stood in front of her bed and said in a stern yet soothing voice, "Joanna, your mother is looking for you. Your mother, Katherine Fines, is looking for you." She stopped screaming and called out for her mother. John made a few calls and within an hour mother and daughter had been reunited. John explained Joanna's situation to her mother, who listened intently to every word that he said.

"She just turned sixteen, Agent Swenson. I was working late and promised her a party the following day, but she snuck out to party with her friends. When I got home from work the following morning, she was gone, and I feared I would never see her again." Sara was up in the room with Joanna and her mother, and Joanna pulled out of her stupor quickly. She only remembered bits and pieces of what had happened to her. She told them about what Clive had done but didn't remember much up until waking in the hospital with John speaking to her. Joanna was going to be fine according to both Sara and Ted. She would need intense psychotherapy, which Sara worked out for her through the hospital, but when John walked out the doors of Northridge that afternoon he knew that he saved that girl from certain death, and he was happy that she was on the road to recovery.

CHAPTER SIXTEEN

The dead guy was on his way to identify himself.

Jessica was swimming in the pool at John's house when Sara walked in from work. She walked out onto the sun deck, and Jessica asked if it was alright that she was swimming. Sara smiled and said it was fine. Jess stayed in the pool as Sara went into the master bedroom to shower and dress for dinner. John was not far behind her, and he headed out to the pool after hearing the splashing, thinking that it was Sara. He walked out onto the sundeck as Jessica was walking out of the water nude, and he stood there dumbfounded and speechless. Jessica smiled and dried herself off, then walked over to the gate off the infinity pool that led down to the beach and stood there looking out at the sunset over the Pacific. John sat down in one of the chairs around a small table and asked, "So, what are your plans now?" Jessica never turned her back from the sea while answering, her perfect nude figure silhouetted against the setting sun. "Sara wants me to go back to school, but I have been out too long for that." "You're still a kid, Jessica. You can go back to high school," John said, sitting admiring the sunset. Sara heard the conversation, and she moved to the foyer that led to the sitting area of the master suite and then out to the pool. She could see Jessica's nude body leaning on the gate down to the beach and John sitting in a chair up on the deck.

"Well, you're a smart girl...too smart for the streets if you ask me. Why not take the GED and go to college?" "Don't know what I want to study." "You can sort that out once you start." "I make more money hooking than I would make in college. Though now that you mention it, I suppose I could hook and go to college." John sat looking out as the sun was beginning to set into the sea and asked, "Why on earth would you want to stay in that life? Sara could help you go as far as possible in academia. The sky is the limit for a young woman as smart as you." "I like it!" That response took John by surprise, and Sara had moved to a chair in the bedroom where she could see the two of them and listen to the conversation, but they couldn't see her. "Come up here and sit down," John said to Jessica in a stern voice. She dropped the towel down to her side, still holding it in her hand, and walked up to the table and sat down. John had a stern look on his face as the automatic lights came on as the darkness began to settle in. Jessica's nipples were hard, and he could see she was covered in goose bumps. He also knew that she was trying to seduce him.

He got up and grabbed a thick terrycloth robe from a clothes rack next to the table and threw it to her. "Put the damn robe on. You're freezing your ass off … and you can't seduce me." Jessica took the robe and put it on, leaving it open so her breasts were exposed and said, "How do you know? You haven't given me a chance!" John laughed and said, "You're a kid. When I look at you, that's what I see. You might have the body of an adult, but you are still a kid. I have been in law enforcement for a lot of years. I have been on too many crime scenes where the victims were prostitutes who made a really good living yet still ended up mangled and bloody." She looked at John and said, "You can't scare me. I've been on the streets for years. I've seen those crime scenes, too." John nodded, looking out at the last of the setting sun and pointed to the horizon. "Take a look." Jessica looked out in the direction where he was pointing but saw just the curvature of the Earth and the last hint of the sun. "What am I looking for?" Jessica asked. "It's not what you're looking for; it's what you looking at!" She looked harder, and then looked at John and said, "I don't see anything." John sighed and said, "That's because you are looking past it. You just witnessed your last sunset."

She looked at John hard and said, "No I haven't!" "How can you be so sure?" Jessica was staring at John intently as she responded, "Because I'm young. I have years and years of sunsets." John laughed. "Ah, the spirit of youth. Unfortunately, you are only immortal for a limited time, and that time for you has passed." Jessica sounded both defiant and frightened when she said, "Are you telling me that I'm going to die tonight?" He looked her straight in the eyes and said, "No…I'm telling you that you have no guarantees in life short of death and taxes, kid. That might very well have been the last sunset that you will ever see. You will most likely never know when that last one will come and go, but we are all guaranteed only one thing in life." Jessica sat back in her chair and asked, "And what guarantee is that?" "We will get one final sunrise and sunset." He watched Jessica's face, and he could see the wheels turning. "I suppose I could find a safer form of work." John smiled, "I thought you might rethink your career goals with that logic in mind."

Sara walked out onto the deck and asked what they were talking about, and Jessica said, "Death." "An interesting conversation to be having. What about it?" "John just drew my attention to the fact that death is coming for me, for us all, in its time, and that I could make some better decisions to hold off its clutches a little longer." Sara sat down next to John and put her hands on top of his, "He said all that, did he? Well, if there is anyone who knows more about death than me, it would be my husband. So, you are a stoic?" Jessica looked on and said, "I'm not sure what that means but perhaps." Sara laughed and said, "Have no fear. My husband is a sage. If anyone can teach you of the things of life, he can." Sara was laughing as she told John that he needed to dress for dinner, and that Jim and Barbara would be there soon. He got up and went into the bathroom to shower and dress. "How long will you let me stay with you and John, Sara?" "Long enough for you to get your GED and apply to a local university. I will help with your testing. If required, I will also pay for your education with the agreement that you will not hook anymore, and that you will use your school years to find a career that suits you." Jessica agreed as the doorbell rang.

Sara's assistant announced that Jade Morgan was at the door. "See her in please." Jessica looked at Sara and asked, "Should I leave?" Sara shook her head. "Who is Jade Morgan?" Sara smiled and said, "You can ask her yourself." Jade made her way onto the deck, and the conversation carried on until Jim and Barbara arrived for dinner. Sara left Jessica and Jade in full conversation about what Jade did for a living. Jessica was hanging on Jade's every word. Sara and John were walking out to meet Jim and Barbara when John asked, "Should we leave those two alone together?" Sara smiled and said, "Absolutely. I think that Jessica might just find her calling." John just shook his head as Jim and Barbara waited for the two of them to join them.

The Los Angeles International Airport spans thirty five hundred acres or five square miles of the California coastline, and most of it is patrolled by the airport police department, a division of the LAPD. A blacked out jeep with sand tires tore its way across the beach, running parallel to an under construction runway at LAX. It was pitch black, as was the jeep, and the only way anyone would know that it was there, was if one of the very, very few spotlights were to shine in its direction. The jeep barreled down the beach until it reached a breach in the fence and leapt a small dune landing on the runway. As it moved at fifty to sixty miles per hour, something came flying out of the jeep and landed on the tarmac. Within seconds, the jeep was gone back into the black of the beach and the night.

Steve and Gail's plane landed at LAX at just past ten a.m. They got their luggage off the government issued private jet and walked to a waiting Bureau car. It whisked them off to the Water Front Hotel with no pomp or circumstance. They arrived at the hotel check in, and Gail admired the suite. "My God, Steve, this room is bigger than my apartment in Brooklyn." There was a laugh as the two walked out onto the balcony that overlooked the sea. "What did you do to deserve this kind of attention from the Bureau?" Gail asked as she was staring at the beach below. "I worked hard, honey. I have worked very hard." Gail finished unpacking and asked, "Are you going to call Jim?" He nodded and said, "Shortly. I need to speak to John first." Steve walked off into the office of the suite, and Gail picked up the line and called Barbara. "O'Brian." "Barbara, it's Gail. Steve and I just landed at LAX and settled into our room, well, suite. Do you have time to meet?" Barbara told her about a little coffee shop off the 10 Freeway at 5th Street before it turned onto PCH. She would meet her there in a half hour. Gail asked if she could take a walk, and Steve nodded and waved to her while he was on the phone. She left the hotel for the coffee house. When she got there, she took a seat and waited for Barbara.

Jim had just gotten to his office when he got a call about a body found on an under construction runway at LAX. He was frustrated and said, "Am I the only fuckin' sheriff in this god forsaken fuckin' town? I have deputies. I will send out a team." The voice on the other end of the line was familiar, and Jim asked, "Do I know you?" "We met a little over a year ago, Sheriff. My name is Alex Martel." Jim scratched his head for a second and then said, "Martel with U.S. Customs?" "Yes, sir. I'm not a customs agent anymore. I'm a part of ICE, and I have been assigned to oversee security for the construction of a new runway and some other buildings here at LAX." "Okay...so what the fuck does that have to do with my office?" There was a moment of hesitation, and Martel said, "One of the construction crews found a body here at LAX." "And what the shit does that have to do with my office or me?" "The body is dressed in one of your deputy's uniforms, Sheriff; it's a male officer who has been shot once in the back of the head." Jim was quiet for a movement and then asked, "Where the fuck are you at LAX?" Martel gave him the information, and Jim hung up the phone and called for his CSI team. He also called Jade Morgan and her CSI team before calling John. He jumped into his car, took a cigarette out of his top left pocket, lit it, and snapped his Zippo closed. He spoke to himself as he drove full speed with his lights on and siren blaring, "Who the FUCK would dare hurt one of my deputies?"

It was half past ten a.m., and John had just gotten to his office but had not yet ascended the building when his cell phone rang. "Swenson." "Hey, John. It's Steve. I just got to LA. I wanted to catch up." "No problem, Steve. This is your domain. I'm at the office. You want to stop by?" There was a pause, and Steve said, "Well…I don't really have a car." "Hey, no problem, sir. I will send one to pick you up at your hotel. What's your room number?" There was a long pause before Steve came back and said, "Yea, yea…send me a car. I'm in suite eight fourteen." John told him no problem and hung up. He called the front desk and asked that a car be sent to pick up an important visitor. He was just about to go when Jim called and told him that he needed him and his team at LAX. All he gave John was the location at the airport.

John arrived on scene before Jim. He called and asked that Steve's car be rerouted to LAX, and there was an FBI sedan with blacked out windows pulling up as John stepped out of his truck. Alex Martel was standing off in the distance, and he waved at John as he started to walk toward him. John saw Steve getting out of the sedan, and he walked over to greet him with a handshake and a pat on the shoulder. He released Steve's car to go back to headquarters saying he would take care of him. Steve looked on as a man in uniform that he recognized as an ICE officer approached, and Jim and his team were pulling onto the construction site before Martel was in full view of John. Steve stayed out of the way as Jim jumped out of his car cussing a blue streak in John and Martel's direction. Jim saw Steve right away and for just a moment was at a loss for words. Then he walked on over to John and looked at Steve and asked, "What's this sorry looking piece of shit doing on my crime scene?" He let out a belly laugh and gave Steve a hug, which was reciprocated as Martel made his way to the three men.

John and Martel locked eyes, and John said, "You're an ICE agent now?" Martel nodded. "So, why are we standing on an unfinished runway?" John asked, as Martel pointed in the direction of a group of men and a yellow tarp on the ground. "I called

Sheriff O'Brian as one of the construction teams showed up on the site this morning and discovered the remains of one of Sheriff O'Brian's men." John looked at Jim who shrugged and said, "As far as I know we have no missing men. I called it in on my way out here, and we have no missing personnel as of this morning." The men followed Martel out onto the unfinished tarmac and to the yellow tarp. Martel lifted it, and Jim looked down at the face of the officer and the name tag and shook his head. John looked on and asked, "Do you know him?" Jim shrugged and said, "I know the uniform and the name tag. Captain Luke Davis from our Toluca Lake office." John and Steve looked on, and John said, "I'm sorry, Jim." Jim shrugged and said, "Why? That's not Captain Davis!" The three men stood in silence for a few minutes, and Jim pulled his cell phone off his hip and called a number.

There were a few moments of silence then Jim said, "Luke...Luke, you there?" Jim was quiet for awhile then said, "Hey...I'm glad that you're alive. I have a little problem out here at LAX. What's the problem, you ask? Well, it's quite a fucked up deal. I am standing over a corpse dressed in your uniform with your name tag, badge, and badge number. Are you missing a uniform?" There were a few more moments of silence, and Jim continued, "Not that you know of...well, did you kill anybody in the last twenty four hours and dump the body in your own clothes on an under construction runway here at LAX?" Steve let out a laugh as John looked on. Jim continued, "It's good to know that you didn't kill anyone. You want to make a drive out here to LAX to see if you can ID the guy in your uniform for us? Great. You can't miss us. Take Century Boulevard until you pass the Bradley terminal, and there will be a shitload of cops there to let you in. Okay, great. We will see you in ten minutes."

Jim hung up the phone and looked at everyone staring at him and said, "What? You haven't seen a guy talk to a dead guy before? He's on his way...oh, and by the way, just in case you guys missed it, it's not my fuckin' guy on the ground here ... at least I don't think so." Jim finished off his cigarette, dropped it on the ground, and was putting it out with his shoe when Jade and her team made their way onto the runway. Jim asked, "Um...Jade...did anyone try to stop you and your people from driving out here?" She shook her head while putting on a pair of latex gloves. Jim nodded slowly. "Great...that's just great. You drive out onto an active crime scene before we have even had a chance to start processing it." Jade just shrugged as she lifted the tarp to look at the body. Jim told her to hold tight. The dead guy was on his way to identify himself. She got a confused look on her face and asked John, "Has Jim been drinking?" John nodded and said, "Yea, but he's telling the truth. The guy on the ground is on his way here to try and identify the body with his nametag." Jade walked back to the van and started talking to a couple of her people while she waited for the dead guy. Jim walked back over to Steve and asked, "So, why the fuck didn't you call me to let me know you were coming?" "I wanted to surprise you." Jim looked on at the yellow tarp and said, "Well, I'm just getting all kinds of fuckin' surprises today." Martel was about to say something when Jim saw one of his cruisers pulling onto the dirt and moving in their direction. "Hold that thought, Martel. The dead guy is here, and, hopefully, he can tell us who the corpse is."

Barbara made it to the coffee shop in Santa Monica and was looking for a spot to sit down when she heard Gail's voice. She turned to see her cute little face smiling back at her from behind a cappuccino. Barb smiled and walked over and gave her a big hug. "I wasn't sure when you would get here, so I grabbed a bite." Barbara smiled and walked up to the counter and ordered a coffee then sat down with Gail. There was an awkward silence before Barb finally took a sip of her coffee and asked, "What's going on, Gail? Steve and Jim are two of a kind. They don't take vacations." Gail sat looking down into her cup when Barbara said, "I doubt very much that the answer is in the bottom of that cup." Gail smiled a faint smile and said, "Steve has been missing LA. He's been thinking about retiring. He has over thirty years in, and he wanted to come back to LA." Barbara took a sip of her coffee and asked, "You have no home. Steve took the cash. You told me that, and now Steve wants to uproot a career in Quantico as the head of behavioral science and retire back in LA? I'm sorry, sweetheart, but I'm not buying it... what's really going on?" Gail's eyes started to fill with tears as she tried to drink her beverage. She looked at Barbara and said, "Steve was diagnosed with ALS last week. He's struggling to make sense of all of it; he needed to get away. He needs to be with people that he knows and respects." Barbara got a sad look on her face and said, "I'm so sorry, Gail. Of all the things that you could have told me that's not something that I would ever have expected." The two sat and chatted for nearly an hour before they separated. Gail asked Barbara to please keep the secret. Gail told her that Steve would tell the guys when he was ready. Barbara nodded and the two made a dinner date for the six of them including Sara and John.

Barbara wasted no time. As soon as she was in her car, she called Sara. "Dr. Swenson." "Sara, it's Barbara. Where are you?" "I'm at home. Why?" "Can I stop by right now?" "Of course. Is everything okay?" Barbara sighed and said, "No," and drove on to Sara and John's house.

CHAPTER SEVENTEEN

*"I still think you are both full of shit,
but, hey, you two are the profilers."*

Captain Davis got out of his cruiser and walked up to Jim who was standing with John and Steve. "So, I'm dead, huh?" Jim nodded and walked him over to the yellow tarp and lifted it up. Davis took one look and started to shake his head. He and Jim were talking away from Steve and John, and John noticed that Steve was unusually quiet. "When's the last time you took a vacation, Steve?" "Never." "So, you just decided on a whim that you wanted to come back to the burned out and rebuilding remains of Los Angeles?" "I did have a life here, John, with my wife, Molly, and for a short time with Gail. I'm thinking about rebuilding, and I'm toying with retirement." John shrugged his shoulders and asked, "Why vacation time? You could come out here on official business, and the Bureau would've picked up the tab." Steve laughed. "I'm on vacation, John; the Bureau is still picking up the tab."

Jim walked over with Luke, and John asked, "So, do you two know who the man is?" Luke nodded and told them that he was one of his employees from a side business that he owned. John looked on and asked, "How did he end up with your uniform and, more importantly, a bullet in the back of his skull?" Davis shrugged as did Jim, and John got a more inquisitive look on his face. "What is your side business, Captain?" "I own a construction company in Woodland Hills. I started it after the fires. We have been doing a booming business." John nodded and asked,

"Who is the dead man?" "His name is Owen Werth. He's a foreman. He handles all of the western part of the valley." "How long has Mr. Werth worked for you?" "He's a retired sheriff's deputy. We have been friends our whole lives. He has been working for me since I started the company a few years ago."

John had his tablet out and was recording the conversation. "Can you think of anyone who would want to kill Mr. Werth?" He shook his head. "Have there been any death threats, fights at work, anything that would lead you to believe that someone would want to kill him?" He shook his head. Jim interrupted and asked, "John, I know you're doing your job here, but let's give my friend a break. One of his best friends has been found murdered." John nodded and was about to put his tablet away when he asked, "Just one more question, Captain Davis." "Of course." "How do you figure that Mr. Werth ended up in your uniform on a runway so far from your home?" Luke just shrugged and said, "I have no idea. Owen has been staying with me and my wife for the past month. He and his wife been having some marital issues, and he needed a place to crash." John thanked him and put his tablet away.

Jim walked over to John and asked, "What are you thinking?" John was putting his equipment into his truck and said, "That this is too easy to solve." Jim looked at him hard and asked, "What do you mean?" John laughed and said, "Put two and two together, Jim. Best friend, marriage problems, comes to stay with his buddy while he works things out. Come on. Do I have to draw you a map?" Jim looked at Davis and then back to John, "Why would he put him in his own uniform?" "I'm betting he didn't. I'm betting that Mr. Davis's wife did that after she took care of him because of something he did." Jim looked on and said, "You think this guy raped Luke's wife?" John nodded. "So, you think she killed him?" "No…I think Luke over there killed him and dumped the body in his uniform as a distraction." Jim had a baffled look on his face.

Steve had been listening to the conversation and chimed in. "John's got it right, Jim. This is a killing gone wrong, but I'm not buying the rape scenario. I bet there was a little wife swapping going on that went beyond the consent of the husband, and he came home and caught him with his cock where it shouldn't have been. I would guess that Werth's not the only one dead. Mrs. Davis is probably dead, too." Jim shook his head. "I've known this man my whole life. I'm telling you he would never do something like that." John interrupted and said, "Everyone is a suspect, right?" Jim nodded. "This is an easy case. Just go out and make a house call. Ask to speak to the wife. I have a dollar that says he will admit to the whole thing." Jim looked on. "So, I should just let him go?" Steve and John nodded in unison. "Then go out and visit him this afternoon?" Again, a nod in unison. Jim walked off and Steve said, "It's nice to get a simple case once in a while." John smiled and said,

"Crimes of passion are the easiest. So, do you have dinner plans?" Steve shook his head. "Well then, you and Gail will dine with me and Sara tonight." Steve laughed, "I have a feeling that that is being worked out as we stand here." John smiled and said, "Our wives?" Steve nodded.

Jim walked back over to the two men as Davis was walking off to his car. "Okay, you two smart asses. I let him go. I told Luke that I would need to talk to him more later, and he said any time. I still think you are both full of shit, but, hey, you two are the profilers." Steve laughed and said, "There's not much to profile here, Jim. He's the killer, and I'm going to go out even further on a limb and say that you will never see him alive again." Jim looked on and asked, "What the fuck does that mean?" John said, "What Steve is saying is that your friend will off himself before you ever get out to see him." Jim took out a cigarette and said, "You two are starting to freak me out. I'm going back to my office. Are you headed downtown?" John nodded. Jim lit the smoke and said, "Well, I have a premonition that the three of us will be having dinner tonight!" Steve laughed and said, "Really? That's your best fuckin' guess based on our wives?" Steve walked over to the passenger side of John's truck and said, "I'm certain we will be having dinner tonight. Call us when you learn of your pal's suicide later today."

Steve closed the passenger door, and John walked on to the truck. Jim stood there with the cigarette hanging out of his mouth saying nothing. He walked over to Jade, who was working the scene. He said, "Hey, kid. I have it on pretty good authority that this scene is going to explain itself before the end of the day. Work it up. I'll call you if I get any other leads." She nodded as he drove away.

Sara was sitting on the deck sunbathing when Barbara walked in. Sara was lying nude on her back in the early afternoon sunlight, and Barbara commented on her perfect shape. "It's genetics, Barb, just genetics." "You don't work out or diet and exercise?" Barb asked, sitting down on one of the recliners on the deck. "When would I have time?" Barbara shrugged and said, "I figured being married to a body building God like John you would be an exercise freak like him." Sara shook her head and said, "John has always been the way he is about his body and body building. I tell him he's a freak all the time." That drew a laugh out of Barbara. Sara pulled down her sunglasses and looked at Barbara and said, "I know you didn't come over here to flirt with me. What's up?" Barbara sat for a few extra seconds too long, and Sara sat up on the recliner and asked, "Okay…what's wrong?"

"I had a cup of coffee with Gail Hoffman this morning near her hotel." "Okay." "She told me that she and Steve were out here on vacation. I drew to her attention that Steve takes vacation as often as Jim." Sara smiled and said, "Which is never. Same goes for John." Barbara said, "Gail mentioned ALS. I have heard of it, but I don't know much about it and have never known anyone who had it." Sara got up off the lounge chair and walked over to the table out of the sun and sat down. "What exactly did Gail say about ALS? Who does she know who has it?" Barbara stammered, "I promised to keep it a secret until she wanted to reveal it. Why? How bad is this illness?" Sara got up and grabbed a robe and a bottle of water from the wet bar, offering one to Barbara who accepted. "It's bad, Barbara. It's really, really bad. It's a death sentence."

Barbara's eyes started to well with tears, and she asked, "I don't understand. How is it a death sentence?" Sara spent the next ten minutes explaining the disease to Barbara, and by the time she was finished Barbara was sobbing uncontrollably. "How long do people live with this disease?" she asked while drying her eyes. "It can vary, but the usual life expectancy from diagnosis to death is between two to five years. There are cases of people living much longer than that and even cases where the disease stopped progressing and even reversed, but those are very, very rare cases." Barbara asked if there was any medication to help stop or slow the disease. "There is one drug that has shown promise in extending life expectancy. It was originally approved by the FDA in 1995, and it has only added a few months. But new clinical trials have shown that if the drug is given at diagnosis, it can slow the progression and give the patient more time before progression, or even slow the same. It's called Riluzole. It's not FDA approved yet for early onset only late stage, but every neurologist that I know is using it the second they diagnose a patient, and it has shown promise. Who's sick, Barb? Who has ALS?"

Barbara looked out over the sea and said, "Steve. That's what Gail told me. That's why they are out here. She said Steve is thinking of retiring and moving back to LA." "How long is Gail going to keep this a secret?" Barbara shrugged. "I want to get him over to my hospital. I have some of the best minds in neurology there, and we are doing several clinical trials for ALS. I'm sure Steve has had a second and probably third opinion, but one more won't hurt. We can also see how advanced the disease is and see how much ambulatory time he might have left." Barbara nodded and said, "I hear what you're saying, Sara, but those are decisions that Steve and Gail need to make, not you and me. I promised to keep this a secret. However, I have a feeling Gail and Steve want to have dinner with us tonight to tell us the news." Sara stood up and called for her assistant. "Then we should have dinner in a private environment. We will dine here at the house." Sara made the plans and asked Barbara to clear it with Gail. The two went their separate ways with Sara telling Barbara dinner would be at seven.

Jim had finished up some paperwork in his office, and it was half past two. His cell rang, and it was Barbara. She told him that he needed to clear his calendar. They were having dinner with Steve and Gail at John and Sara's at seven. "And don't fuck around, Jimmy. Get your ass home, so you can shower and change for dinner." "Okay, okay…Jesus Christ. It's Steve and Gail not the fuckin' pope!" He hung up the phone and headed out while deciding to pay a surprise visit to Luke at his home.

Steve and John arrived back at the federal building. Steve was unusually quiet, and John chatted with him going into the building and up to his office. They were walking past the bullpen of field agents, and Steve stopped for a second to look around outside the first office he put John in when he hired him away from the LAPD. John stopped and looked at Steve's face and asked, "Are you okay, Steve?" He nodded. "I just had a moment. I remember when I hired you. I dumped the Iron Eagle case on you, and you took it like a trooper." "A lot of water has passed under that bridge." Steve nodded as they walked on toward John's office. He invited Steve to sit, which he did. Steve stumbled a few times walking to John's office, and John caught it but didn't say anything. When they were settled, John asked, "So, Special Agent Steve Hoffman is on vacation. The special agent that I have never known to take a day off in the years that I have known him. What's up?"

Steve looked around the office that was once his. John could see that Steve was in another world, and he let him be for several minutes. When he finally looked like he was back, John asked, "Where are you?" Steve looked around and said, "I haven't been home in a lot of years. I can't tell you how many sleepless and sleeping nights I spent in this office behind the very desk you're sitting at, working cases, trying to figure out who was behind some of the most horrific crimes of the twentieth and twenty first century." John smiled and asked, "Are you still obsessing over the Iron Eagle?" "Of course. He's still out there, John. We have a whole department at Quantico dedicated to working on the Eagle. We have had little luck though." "How so?" "You know I'm not a conspiracy guy, but since the Hernandez situation last year and his reelection, the administration has cut our budget for several pet projects, like searching for the Eagle. I know Hernandez has a reverence for the guy, but he's still a cold-blooded killer, and he has to be stopped." John sat back and said, "Perhaps the Eagle is doing the world a favor?" Steve stood up and paced the room, looking out the window over Westwood.

"Yea…that's what the world seems to think. John, I've been in behavioral science for my entire career. While the Eagle may be doing what some people condone as right in his vigilante activities, psychologically there is a fine line between the logical avenging of crimes and murder." John looked on and said, "Are you saying the Eagle will cross some line?" Steve nodded. "I am, and it's not an if, it's a when. When will the Eagle cross the line from vigilante killer to simple cold- blooded serial killer?" "You don't think that the Eagle can tell the difference?" John asked nonchalantly. "I'm telling you that the Eagle will cross from being one thing to another without even knowing he has done it!" The look on Steve's face was serious, and John could see the concern.

John said, "Not to change the subject, but are you feeling okay?" Steve said, "Yea. Why do you ask?" "Did you hurt your right leg?" Steve had a confused look on his face. "I strained my hamstring a few days ago running up the stairs to my office. It's still a little weak and sore. It will be fine." John looked on and said, "I received a text from Sara. You and Gail are having dinner at our home tonight with Jim and Barbara." Steve smiled and said that sounded nice. John sat for a few more minutes then asked, "Tell me about that hammy you pulled on the stairs a few days ago. I have never known you to be one for running anywhere unless you were being chased." "I pulled a muscle, John. For God's sake. Are you going to make a federal case out of it?" John didn't miss a beat. "No, but I've seen that type of walk before. In a friend of mine, years ago, and it turned out not to be a sore muscle. It was something else." Steve sat back in his chair and asked, "Okay, mister clairvoyant, what do my pulled hammy and your friend have in common?" John's face was grave, and he looked at Steve and said, "In the case of my friend, it was a symptom of a much more sinister disease." "Enlighten me." "Have you gone to the doctor to make sure it's just a pulled tendon?" Steve didn't respond; he just stared out the office window. John watched and could see that Steve was detached. John could tell that Steve wanted to talk about everything and anything other than the subject he came to talk to John about.

John sat quiet for a few moments then broke the silence and said, "You're not on vacation, Steve. You're here because you're sick!" Steve never took his eyes off the window. Instead, he stood up, walked over, and put his hands on the windowsill and said, "In all of my years in this office I never realized that my office window looked out over a veteran's cemetery. I mean, I always knew it was there. I just never gave any mind to the fact that the constant specter of death wasn't just on the cork boards of my inner office; it was the view I looked out on every day." John sat silent. Steve still had his back to John and was staring out the window. "I was just diagnosed with ALS." John didn't say anything, but the look on his face when Steve turned around told him that he already knew. Steve sat back down in the chair and asked, "But I haven't told you anything. You didn't already know." John's eyes were starting to tear up, and Steve watched the giant of a man sit silent at his desk as a tear trickled out the corner of his right eye." John spoke softly, "I'm sorry, Steve." "Me, too, John. Me, too." "I assume that Gail knows?" Steve nodded. "Have you told Jim?" Steve shook his head. "Why not?" Steve took a deep breath with tears in his eyes and said, "I don't know how to do it." John smiled a teary smile and said, "Just tell him. Jim's a tough guy. He can handle it." The two men sat in silence, both looking out the window until Steve asked, "Will you take a walk with me?" John nodded, and the two men took the elevator down to the ground floor. Steve started across the parking lot of the federal building he had worked in for nearly two decades and crossed Wilshire to the veteran's cemetery, and he and John walked among the tombstones in silence.

CHAPTER EIGHTEEN

"Fuck...maybe I have Alzheimer's and don't know it?"

Jim arrived at Luke's house just off of Victory Boulevard in Winnetka in the San Fernando Valley at a little before three. The property was a sprawling estate. In looking around, Jim figured that Luke must have bought up a bunch of the lots from his neighbors or their estates, if they had them, to take up so much property in a city that put a premium on space. He knocked on the front door and called out, but there was no response. He grabbed the door handle, and it was unlocked. Since he and Luke went back a lifetime, he walked in and called out to him and his wife, Cheryl, but there was no answer. He walked around the house until he made it to the kitchen. Breakfast was still on the table. There were pans on the stove and a woman's robe draped across the back of one of the dining room chairs. He looked around and said, "I'm starting to get a bad fuckin' feeling." He heard the sound of an engine running, and he walked over and opened the door that led into a garage.

The fumes were too heavy for him to get through, so he closed the door and called 911 and his team. He knew who was in the garage and what had happened. He ran through the house calling for Cheryl, but there was no response. The house was a sprawling ranch style home, and he searched room by room as he heard the sound of sirens approaching in the distance. He made it to the back of the house and flung open a door to see that it was the master bedroom. Cheryl Davis was lying in bed covered up, and he walked over carefully to check on her when he saw blood on the wall near where her head was. He checked her for a pulse, but there was none, and she was cold. He walked out of the bedroom and out the front door to his car. He pulled out a CSI kit from the trunk, put on a pair of latex gloves, and walked over to the garage. He put his shirt over his mouth as he opened the door and felt for the opener on the wall. He found a button and pushed it, and the door began to rise. He stepped back into the kitchen and then went out the front door and over to the garage to see a black Jeep with a hose in its tail pipe leading into the driver side window. As he walked up to the Jeep, an ambulance pulled up in front of the house just ahead of the fire department and his team. Jim reached into the vehicle and turned off the ignition. There, in the driver's seat, was Luke Davis. Jim checked for a pulse, but there was none.

He walked to the curb and took a moment as his team pulled up and unloaded their equipment. He waved his hand in the air while leaning over with his hands on his knees. "Come here, you assholes. Come here! This is not going to be a complicated case. This is a murder suicide. I have known the man who is dead in that garage my entire life. His wife is in bed with a single gunshot wound to the head. The wife is Cheryl Davis, and the dead man is retired Sheriff's Captain Luke Davis. I'm sure there will be a note. This crime scene is related to the one at LAX this morning. I'm sure the note will explain it all. I'm going to leave the scene and call Special Agent Swenson and Special Agent Hoffman and thank them for their ESP abilities. Write it up, but this is an open and shut case."

Jim walked off to his car. He stopped and took out a cigarette, lit it, and took a couple of deep drags. As he leaned on the open driver's door he said, "Mother fucker...shit... Luke. How the fuck could you do that to Cheryl? Jesus Christ, man. Jesus fuckin' Christ." Jim got into the car and sped off down the street back to his office downtown. He had his phone in his hand with John's cell number on speed dial, but he threw the phone onto the seat next to him and said, "Fuck the two of them. I'm not going to give them the satisfaction of knowing they were right, at least not yet."

There was a note from Barbara on the kitchen table for Jim when he got home a little before six.

"I'm over at Sara's. Take off your clothes, start the shower, get into the shower, pick up the soap, wash your body with the soap. Wash your hair, shave, then dry off. I put clothes out for you on the bed. When you are dressed, come over to John and Sara's.

Love,

Your Bitchy Ball and Chain"

Jim threw the note on the table and said, "Jesus. Am I a fuckin' kid who has to be told everything in order to bathe?" He walked back to the master bedroom where Barbara had laid out his clothes. He started the shower, and there were little sticky notes from Barbara all over the bathroom. "Fuck...maybe I have Alzheimer's and don't know it?" He showered and shaved then dressed and decided to walk over to John and Sara's since it was a nice evening, and they only lived a few blocks away. "No sense in having two cars there, assuming Barb drove." He set out for John's house walking along PCH in the cool evening air. The fog was blowing in off the ocean, and the salty smell of the sea air was refreshing to his lungs as he took deeper and deeper breaths. Jim stopped just before turning on to John's property and took a moment to listen to the surf crashing off in the distance. He drew another deep breath and said, "At least this fuckin' day can't get any worse or more bizarre."

Sara and Barbara were sitting in the living room when Jim came in. They were drinking wine and chatting on one of the sofas. Jim walked in and looked down at his PDA to see that it was just seven p.m. "Okay...I'm here, you guys are here, where are Steve, Gail, and John?" Sara hushed him and asked if he wanted a drink. "Scotch, neat and tall. I've had one hell of a day!" Sara poured it for him, and he sat down next to Barbara. John entered the foyer dripping with sweat. He was in nothing but a pair of shorts that were way too small for him with a pair of weight lifting gloves on. He was almost purple, and the veins were bulging through the surface of his skin on his arms, legs, and chest. Jim took one look at him and said, "Christ, man, are you having a heart attack?" John shook his head, "Just got done with a workout after weight lifting." Jim took a drink of his scotch watching the looks on both Sara and Barbara's faces, looks of lust, and asked, "Weight lifting isn't enough of a workout...what the fuck? Were you running on the beach?" John nodded and left the room. Jim looked at Sara and asked, "That's all natural?" She nodded smiling. "I don't care what any of you say that is steroid enhanced."

Jim had finished saying it when it was announced that Steve and Gail had arrived. They were shown into the formal living room where Sara and her guests were seated. Steve was looking around in awe as was Gail. Steve looked at Sara and asked, "This is from your inheritance from that Cruthers guy?" She nodded. Gail asked, "How big is your home?" Sara smiled and said, "That depends on whether you want the square footage that John and I actually live in or the overall." "The overall," said Gail. "Um...several hundred thousand, but John and I only use about five thousand on a regular basis." Sara poured them each a drink and told them that John would be along shortly. There was quiet chit chat, which Jim picked up right away as wrong. John walked in, and Sara gave him a glass of wine. "I thought you didn't drink?" Steve asked. "A few things have changed over the past few years, but I don't drink with regularity."

Steve shook his head as the conversation wore on. It was Jim who finally sat back and asked, "What the fuck is going on here?" Barb didn't make a sound. She knew Jim was going to figure things out sooner rather than later. There were a few moments of silence, and Steve asked, "What?" Jim took a swig of his drink and said, "We don't make idle chit chat. We never have. Why are you here, Steve? And don't give the 'I'm on vacation' bullshit. I know you better than that." The room was silent, and Jim could tell by the long faces in the room that whatever the reason for Steve's visit, it was not pleasure. Steve took a drink of his beverage and said, "You're right. I'm not here on vacation, Jim. I'm here because I was diagnosed just about a week ago with ALS."

Tears started flowing from all in the room except John. Jim stared at Steve for a long time before he responded. "If this is a fuckin' joke, it's not funny, and if it's the truth it's not mother fuckin' fair!" Jim said it with such conviction that the women broke into tears. John looked at Jim and said, "It's the latter, Jim." Jim stood up, walked over to the bar, and poured another drink. He sat back down next to Barbara and started talking like he had not just heard what he did from Steve. "You two clairvoyants were right about Luke. I found my childhood friend dead in his Jeep this afternoon. Jade called me about an hour ago to tell me that they found his suicide note admitting to everything that you two predicted. Congratulations on solving a case without ever putting on a pair of gloves." He toasted the two men as the room was quiet except for a few sniffles from the girls. Steve looked over at Jim and asked, "Did you hear what I just told you?" Jim nodded and said, "I'm sorry, Steve...I'm really fuckin' sorry. Just when I thought this day couldn't get any worse, it just did. You know that there isn't a damn thing I can do to help you, medically. That's Sara's department. So how much functional time have the doctors given you?"

"It's hard to say. Two to five years is the normal life span." Jim laughed taking a swig of his drink. "Well, if there's one thing I know about you, there ain't nothing normal about your ass." That got a faint laugh from all in the room. "So, what now...you going to pack it in and head for some beach somewhere and fuck Gail day and night until you can't fuck no more?" Gail laid her head on Steve's shoulder as he answered, "Well, yes. At some point before this disease takes me, I'm going to take Gail on a long vacation, but my plan is to come back out here to LA and work for a few months." Jim and John stared at each other. John asked,

"One, why would you want to come back here, and, two, why the hell would you want to work?" Steve sat back in his seat and said, "My doctor told me that there is a clinical trial at UCLA that I can enroll in. I can have Sara as my primary care physician, if she will accept the job." Sara nodded empathically.

"They have me on a drug that is not FDA approved for early onset ALS, but I'm on it anyway, and I figure if I'm going to take the trip, why not try to help a few folks if I can through medicine. And since I'm going to be here as a guinea pig, I see no reason to sit on my sorry ass, so I will work cases with Jim and your dumb ass until either I feel it's time for that last trip with Gail or my doctors and Sara tell me it's time to do it." There was a moment of silence, and Jim let out a laugh. "Why the fuck not? You're dead anyway. You look good, and you're still able to move around. Who knows? You might get lucky and catch a bullet before this damn disease gets you." John nodded as did the girls, and they spent the rest of the night talking about the plans for Steve to take office space back in LA and to work cases with John and Jim, if necessary. The conversation turned so matter of fact about normal things that for a few hours Steve and Gail felt a sense of normalcy again. And the room was light as if nothing serious was happening. That the specter of death was not hanging over Steve…for the moment.

DEVIL'S CHAIR

The Iron Eagle Series: Book Six

PROLOGUE

The road was broken and tattered beneath the wheels of Swenson's pickup truck as he and Steve Hoffman drove off road after leaving Angeles Crest Highway, better known as Highway 2 just outside of LA. It was half past three a.m. and neither man spoke as John drove down the dirt and blacktop road to the Devil's Punchbowl. They were headed to a remote location only a mile or so from the small town of Devil's Chair in the Los Angeles Forest. The road slash trail was pitch black ahead of them as they drove at a nearly seventy-degree angle downhill. Steve didn't even challenge John when it came to remote locations; this was the third trip to this part of the county in two months. He trusted that John knew what he was doing. The darkness was suddenly flooded with the lights of police and fire ahead of them. As they approached, they were guided to the side of the road by a sheriff's deputy with a flashlight who was yelling at the top of his lungs, "WHO THE FUCK DO YOU THINK YOU ARE? WHAT ARE YOU DOING ON THIS ROAD?"

He looked in to see John and Steve wearing their FBI wind breakers and fell silent. John parked the truck, and the two men walked toward the lights. Steve looked over at John and said, "One day soon I will be hearing the words, 'go to the light.'"

John smiled a half-hearted smile as the two men made it to a small gully where Jim O'Brian was standing with a cigarette in one hand and a flashlight in the other, yelling down a small ravine at someone unseen. "Another body?" Steve asked casually. Jim turned around and saw them standing behind him in their bright blue windbreakers and said, "No, Steve. No. It's not that…I got you two assholes out of bed because there is a mother lode of fuckin' gold down there, and I didn't want you to miss out!" Jim's radio crackled, and John recognized the voice on the radio right away. "That's Jade…where is she?" Jim pointed into the darkness and said, "She's so loaded down with that gold I was telling you about that she's just out of her mind."

Steve threw his hands in the air signaling enough from Jim who took a hit off his smoke and said, "She's down with two bodies discovered by hikers earlier this evening." John looked on and asked, "Don't you have a chopper with night sun to help out?" Jim shook his head and said, "Budget cuts. Thank the asshole governor. Since this is not a search and rescue, they won't let us use it." John took his phone off his hip and called out for a chopper. They were looking down the ravine, and John grabbed the rope and started to repel down to meet up with Jade. Steve stood with Jim staring down into the black. Jim looked at Steve and asked, "Too weak?" Steve shook his head. "Too fuckin' old. That shit is a young man's game." He had no sooner said it when the sound of chopper blades broke the otherwise silent scene, and a night sun shined down onto a horrific terrain.

Jim looked at Steve and said, "Show off." Steve smiled looking down at John and Jade in the gully. Near them were what appeared to be human remains, but they were hard to make out. Jim radioed down and asked, "What do you have down there?" Jade came back and said, "It's hard to tell. Looks like the animals have been having a feast, but the remains appear to be male. It's colder than shit down here, and there is a lot of snow and ice." Jim looked down blowing smoke in Steve's face as he spoke over the radio. "Same as the others?" John came on the radio and said, "Yea, both men, or what's left of them, are nude. They haven't been out here for very long though. There's enough here for Jade to do an autopsy on. It looks like they died from exposure. I think nature had a snack though after they were dead." "Well, get them on a gurney, and we will bag them up here. Since you're already down there, Agent Swenson, you and Jade can work the scene." Jim laughed after he said it, and John came back with a simple, "Roger."

Jim and Steve walked back to the four by four. He looked at Steve, took another cigarette out of his top left pocket and asked, "How you feeling?" Steve was half yelling over the sound of the chopper. "Pretty good, actually. It's a bitch that I will most likely die before you. You smoke those goddamn cigarettes." Steve laughed as Jim lit up and said, "Hey…it's not a race. It's a marathon. You don't know. I could take the trip before you. Between you and me, since you have been back working with John and me these past three months, I think you are doing better. I think you got a lot of years left in you." Steve smiled and said, "Sara keeps me on the experimental drugs and other medications for fatigue and muscle spasms, but you and I know I'm in a race against time that I won't win." Jim nodded as the gurneys were being pulled up by the sheriff's department's urban search and rescue.

"Ironic huh…" Jim pointed to the search and rescue on his deputy's uniform. Everyone on scene was bundled up against the January morning. The temps were in the single digits at that elevation, and Jim laughed at Steve shivering on the half frozen mountain road and said, "It's a bitch, ain't it? You move from Virginia for the California warmth, and you end up spending the California winter in the goddamn mountains." Steve nodded as the last body was brought up then waited for John and Jade to emerge. It was about four thirty when they pulled themselves up out of the ravine with several bags of evidence. "Homicide?" Steve asked. Jade and John looked at each other then at Steve and Jim. Jade said, "I need to get them on the table, but I don't think so. There are no signs of trauma outside of where the animals were eating." Steve watched as the chopper cleared the area. The scene fell more silent, and he said, "Jesus Christ! What the fuck is going on out here? Five bodies differing in age found between Devil's Chair and the Devil's Punchbowl in two months, and none of them are homicides. "Some sick suicide pact?" Jim asked. John and Steve shrugged as Jade walked off to make sure the remains ended up in the right van.

Adam Osborn had just arrived at his office in Irvine when Gaston Reed walked in and sat down. "Gaston, it's ten after eight. Can it wait?" "No it can't, Adam. You know goddamn well that I have been working with Wallace Foods for six months on cooking a deal, no pun intended, to sell our products in the south." Adam nodded as he opened Outlook on his computer. "So, what's this I hear about Beatrice Hanks closing the deal? This deal is mine, Adam. You know that." "It's yours, Gaston. Beatrice is working with a whole different division of that company. She closed a deal that has nothing to do with you and your deal, and it's not worth near the money you are going to make in commissions on yours." "You better be telling me the truth, Adam, or there will be blood!" He stormed out of Adam's office, and Adam knew trouble was brewing. He picked up the phone and called HR and asked for Amelia Farrell.

"Amelia, I know it's early, and it's Monday, but we have a problem. Gaston is having a shit fit over a deal that Beatrice made, and for the second time in a week he's stormed out of my office claiming 'there will be blood' if he loses a deal. I am just reporting it to you as it is now Rollins Industries' policy to report workplace threats." There were a few thanks exchanged, and he hung up and started his day.

Gaston Reed got the call to come to HR before ten, and he cursed under his breath as he headed for Amelia's office. "I knew I should have kept it together. They're going to call it a threat, and I'm going to get canned." He walked on to HR where Amelia was waiting for him in the hall. Not three minutes went by, and Gaston was being escorted to his car with the belongings from his office in a box. He was screaming obscenities and threats as he was escorted off the premises.

Amelia let Adam know what had been done, so he could keep an eye on his back, but he had had hundreds of people fired through the years and nothing ever came of the threats. He finished up for the day and was happy for what Beatrice was able to do. He closed up his office at just after seven and walked out to his car escorted by security just as a safety precaution. He was going to meet Beatrice and Amelia for a drink but decided to stop off at home to change out of his suit. He had a nice one bedroom condo in a high rise condo complex in downtown Irvine. It suited his single lifestyle well. He got to his building and buzzed in, got to his unit where he quickly changed clothes, and then darted out to meet the others. He pulled out of the parking structure, but there was construction, so he turned the opposite direction on North Lake Drive and headed for the lake itself. He figured he could cut back up to Lake Side Drive and head out.

He looked at the clock on the dash, and it showed eight thirty p.m. He sat stopped, alone, when he noticed a pair of headlights behind him. He made a few turns headed for the bar, and the car stayed right behind him. He started to panic when he saw the bar and turned in and parked. He ran in a panic only to see the dark car behind him drive on past his location at a fast pace. He calmed down and had drinks with his coworkers. It was just after ten when they said their good nights and went their separate ways. Adam was feeling good. He had been checked out by the bartender and was under the legal limit to drive, so he made his way to his car. He was just about to enter when a hand grabbed him from behind, and he felt a sharp pain between his shoulder blades. He lost consciousness almost immediately.

When he came to, he was in a dark room. He could feel cold steel against his back, and he tried to move but couldn't. There was a very low red light on over his head, and he could see his clothes on the floor not far from where he lay. "You, my friend, are a liar and a thief." The voice was not familiar to Adam, and he looked around wildly. "Who are you?" Adam yelled into the empty room. "Your executioner." "Gaston…is that you?" Silence met the question. Adam heard the sound of a motor somewhere in the darkness. It started off slow but sped up until it was the familiar sound of a band saw. Adam was freaking out and screaming, "Gaston...Gaston...if this is your doing, I'm sorry. I really meant no harm. You made threats. There was nothing I could do."

Adam felt his body start moving on the steel unit he was laying on. His right shoulder was turned out, and his back was pressed against the cold steel. The red light got brighter and soon he could see an industrial band saw in front of him. He could see wood shavings on the ground, and he cried out again, only there was no reply as he saw a piece of his right shoulder fall to the floor after the saw blade passed through it. He let out a scream, and the table moved back again, cutting more of his flesh. Adam called out to God. His captor laughed through the darkness and said, "I'm sorry, Adam. God's not listening tonight." As the blade passed through Adam's right side again, he tried to move but was restrained and blood was pouring out of his wounds. A large circular saw blade began to rotate under the middle of the table, and the table moved forward as Adam screamed, and the blade bore its way through his groin splitting his body in two. Adam fell silent.

His captor walked over to his dead body. His white coat and pants glowed in the eerie red light. He put on a hard hat and said, "I told you God wasn't listening, Adam; however, if God exists, I bet you're chatting him up right now." There was a quiet laugh as the man wheeled Adam's body through a set of double doors and into a bright light.

About the Author

Roy A Teel Jr. is the author of several books, both nonfiction and fiction. He became disabled due to Progressive Multiple Sclerosis in 2011 and lives in Lake Arrowhead, CA with his wife, Tracy, their tabby cat, Oscar, and their Springer Spaniel, Sandy.

CPSIA information can be obtained at www.ICGtesting.com
Printed in the USA
LVOW07*2002310815

452277LV00001B/2/P